Brad's gaze landed on her nails.
He stared. And stared.

"Coral."

Callie's comment visibly jarred him.

"The polish." She wiggled her fingers. "You like it?"

With a blank stare, he said, "As you can see, we serve coffee and donuts here, so if you skip going to the bakery, you might actually get here on time."

Her happy day paled a bit.

"Is it the nail polish? Admittedly not a great color for me."

He said nothing.

"I'll skip my trip to the bakery in the morning," Callie said.

"So, you'll be here by eight-thirty tomorrow morning, right?" Noticeable edge to his voice there.

"Right."

"Good." He then explained the program to her, but she didn't hear a word of it. She couldn't image how this rude, arrogant man was the same suave, debonair man she'd met at the bakery that morning. She couldn't believe she'd given up a perfectly good peach scone for this guy. It wouldn't happen again.

Books by Diann Hunt

Love Inspired

Hearts Under Construction
Hometown Courtship

Previously published under the pseudonym Diann Walker

Love Inspired

A Match Made in Bliss
Blissfully Yours

DIANN HUNT

Bestselling author Diann Hunt writes romantic comedy and humorous women's fiction. She admits to seeing the world from a slightly different angle than most, and she will do just about anything (within reason) for chocolate. Since 2001, she has published three novellas and fifteen novels, including a Women of Faith novel.

Diann lives in Indiana with her real-life hero-husband of 33 years who continually lavishes her with chocolate—well, she can imagine it, can't she? She's a fiction writer, after all.

Hometown Courtship
Diann Hunt

**Steeple
Hill**®

Published by Steeple Hill Books™

STEEPLE HILL BOOKS

Steeple
Hill®

Recycling programs
for this product may
not exist in your area.

ISBN-13: 978-0-373-81417-6

HOMETOWN COURTSHIP

Copyright © 2009 by Diann Hunt

www.SteepleHill.com

Printed in U.S.A.

Trust in the Lord with all your heart
and lean not on your own understanding;
in all your ways acknowledge him,
and he will make your paths straight.

— *Proverbs* 3:5–6

Dedicated to my Lord and Savior, Jesus Christ,
who continually guides my steps.

Special thanks to my editor, Tina Colombo, for her
hard work and for joining me with this project! I
am blessed to be a part of the Love Inspired team!

Chapter One

The strike of the judge's gavel reverberated through the room, announcing to the entire town of Burrow, Ohio, that she, Callie Easton, had committed a crime. She could almost see the stern glares of the city's forefathers.

Who knew that lost parking tickets could cause such a problem?

Heather Rinker, Callie's good friend and attorney, leaned toward her. "You okay?"

"I've just been ordered to do community service, Heather. Would you be okay?"

"No, but then I don't lose things." She gathered her copious papers into tidy little stacks and placed them in her folder.

"It's the handbag. I wouldn't be in this mess if not for the handbag." Callie hiccupped. Her usual reaction to life's crises.

Heather turned to her. "What?"

"It was on sale. I love the smell of leather—did I ever tell you that?—and this leather bag looked so cute. It was the right price, and—"

Heather sighed and tucked her file carefully into her portfolio. "Callie—"

"—it has a million pockets, Heather. Pockets, where things are stored, never to be found again." Callie slumped further into her chair, trying to swallow past the shame that had settled rock solid in her throat. "What am I going to do? Aunt Bonnie needs me."

"Look, Cal—"

"Do you think if I told the judge that spring is one of the busiest seasons of the year for our salon that he would pick another time? I mean, since I'm not a big-city crime boss and all." She bit her lower lip. "This is an awful time to desert Aunt Bonnie." Callie rubbed her aching temples. "Why don't they just fine me or something?"

"This is how it's done in Burrow, Callie." A flicker of sympathy lit Heather's eyes. A rare occurrence, indeed.

"Any chance you could ask him to reconsider?" Callie asked.

"You're kidding, right?" Heather picked up her leather briefcase and started to briskly walk toward the door. To others, her five-foot-two frame may have looked dainty in her smart beige suit and fashionable heels, but Callie knew that inside that petite body lurked the strength of a five-hundred-pound prison matron. She was sheer grit and discipline, that one. How the two of them could be such great friends was a mystery to everyone who knew and loved them.

A new set of witnesses and onlookers shuffled inside the court, tingeing the air with the scent of stale tobacco and sweet perfumes.

Putting all self-respect behind her, Callie slung her handbag over her shoulder, hauled her five-foot-seven self after Heather, practically jogging to keep up, and said—between great heaving breaths—"No, I'm not kidding."

Heather stopped dead center in front of Callie and point-blank stared her in the face. Her friend's eyes turned positively beady.

"It's the price you pay for losing your parking tickets."

Heather turned and headed into the hallway. Callie continued her jog to keep up. "That was harsh, Heather. Even for you." Three gum wrappers slipped from an outside pocket of Callie's handbag and drifted to the floor. She picked them up, stuffed them into the nearest hole in her bag and shifted the strap on her shoulder.

"It's what I've been telling you, Cal. You have

to get organized. You can't afford to lose important documents."

Pockets. She had to stay away from pockets and nasty little corners where important papers could hide. She'd better dump out her handbag when she got home and take a look. Who knew what else lurked there.

"Aunt Bonnie, Heather. You know she needs me—especially during prom season. You know how you love her peach scones? She'd make you some if—"

Heather stopped, horror on her face. "Are you trying to bribe me?"

"Well, no, I don't think so. I just thought—"

"Well, don't think. Just do your duty as a good citizen—"

"Please don't make me do this over a couple of old parking tickets." Callie suddenly realized she had been reduced to groveling. Could life get any worse?

"Seven old parking tickets."

"There it is. The ugly truth in all its glory." Callie sighed.

Heather placed a hand on Callie's shoulder. "Look, I know this is tough for you and you're worried about the salon, but it will be over soon and you can get back to business. Hopefully, you'll learn how to get a bit more organized in the process."

"So, I really have to build a house?"

Heather chuckled. "Well, not single-handedly."

Callie could practically smell the sawdust, and for a moment, she was ten years old, staring up at her dad. He took off his tool belt and hard hat and laid them on the kitchen table. Pulling her into his arms, he said, "I'll always love you, Beanie." He brushed away a tear from his face, gave her one last squeeze and walked out the door. Callie flung herself at him, crying, grabbing at the door to get to him while her aunt and uncle held her back, embracing her until she'd shed every last tear.

"Hey, you all right?"

Callie's eyes refocused on Heather's concerned expression. Now was not the time to revisit her father's leaving after her mom died—she had to get out of this situation. "Will I have to wear a tool belt? Please say no. I just couldn't live with myself."

Heather stared at her a little too long and finally said, "You make me crazy, you know that? I gotta go." Her heels clacked across the shiny tiled floor as she went to the courthouse doors.

"What if I toss the handbag?" It was a last-ditch effort that Heather ignored as she disappeared through the door, but Callie figured it couldn't hurt to try.

She hated letting her aunt down this way. Thirty years old and still irresponsible. And building a house was exactly what she didn't need. Old memories were better left buried.

"It's your fault," she growled at the handbag. Shrugging it into place on her shoulder, Callie shoved through the courthouse doors and swept down the steps toward her car. She could think of better ways to start the weekend.

"This car belong to you?" Another man in a blue uniform. Were they stalking her or what?

Callie stopped in front of her car, and with one glance at the empty meter, considered telling a fib. Her upbringing wouldn't allow it. "Yes."

He ripped a ticket from his thick, neat little pad. "Looks like this belongs to you, too." He smiled, tipped his hat and walked away.

If she could put her parking tickets in an organized pad like that, she wouldn't even *be* at the courthouse. Grumbling, she climbed inside her car, then crammed her ticket deep into her handbag. She'd deal with that later.

"I can't believe you're doing this to me again." Brad Sharp walked off the concrete foundation, away from listening ears. He growled into the phone, "Listen, Ryan, you remember what a disaster the last community servant was for the Make a Home project? She went through every nail in the county before we could finish the framing. And then there was the other one. *She* was a honey. Decided to hijack the Bobcat and splintered our framing wood into a thousand pieces." His voice rose with anger. "I can't afford your community servants, bro."

Ryan wasn't ruffled in the least. "So we've had a few clunkers. It's a worthy cause. And you're into worthy causes, after all."

Brad could hear the teasing in Ryan's voice and it irritated him. "Isn't this called abusing your position of power?" His work boots stomped over mounds of clumped dirt on the job site. Nails jostled in his tool belt. Behind him men unloaded lumber from the truck to prepare for framing. Workers called out to one another. Saws whirred, spitting flakes of dust into the spring air. He had a job to do and didn't have time for this.

"I don't see it that way. Callie Easton needs to serve the community, and you are heading up a community project, building a brand new house for a Burrow family." Pages turned. No doubt Ryan was scanning his next case while talking. "Besides, this is a win-win situation."

"Oh, sure. Dump a perp on me and you can strike your gavel without another thought. What did she do, anyway?"

"She didn't pay her parking tickets."

Brad stopped in his tracks. "You're kidding."

"Would I kid about the law?"

"And I'll bet she's single and in her early thirties, am I right?"

Silence.

Brad groaned. "Come on, Ryan. This isn't about justice. This is about you wanting me to settle down. Why is it you married men aren't happy unless you take all your single buddies down with you?"

"Hey, marriage is a great institution. Don't knock it till you've tried it."

"Look, I'm glad for you and Brianna, but it's not for me. You know that. I don't need a wife to tie me down."

"*Au contraire,* little brother. I think that's exactly what you need. Find a good woman, settle down in Burrow."

"Don't start, Ryan. I'm not like you. I don't want to stay here forever. A woman won't change that."

It was true that Ryan was a big-name judge and Brad was merely a carpenter, but that didn't give Ryan the right to plan out Brad's life for him. The last thing he would ever do was get involved with a woman his brother had chosen for him.

"Why are you always so closed to everything I say?"

"You never hear me. I've told you a million

times I want to keep working abroad, not stay holed up in Burrow, Ohio. I'm only here until I get my next assignment in South America."

"I can think of worse things." Ryan's voice had an edge to it this time.

"I'm not saying it's a bad thing. It's just a bad thing *for me*. I'm wired differently than you. Why can't you accept that?"

Ryan sighed. "I'm sorry I upset you, Brad. We'll talk later. Callie starts Monday."

The line went dead and Brad snapped his cell phone shut. "Great, that's just great."

He knew his brother meant well, but Brad wished that just once Ryan would let him run his own life.

Monday morning came much too soon. Callie was thankful at least that Jessica Moore had agreed to work full-time at the salon until Callie was through "serving time." Jessica was the other stylist at the salon. As a rule, Jessica worked part-time so she could take some classes and care for her mom, who had been through a major surgery. But her mom was getting better and her classes were coming to an end, so Jessica offered to help Callie out.

Thunder boomed across the morning sky, causing Callie's red VW to tremble slightly. She peered through her rain-pelted car window. "Oh, this is just perfect."

With a grunt she reached for her red-and-white polka-dotted umbrella, slammed the door of her car and ran into the Peaches & Cream Bakery.

Though she was running late, of course, she wasn't about to give up her coffee and peach scone. It had nothing to do with her aunt and uncle owning the place. The bakery was known across the county for its delicious peach pastries—hence, the name. It could be a bit confusing to tourists—they owned the Peaches & Cream Bakery, the Peaches & Cream Salon and the Peaches & Cream Ice Cream Parlor.

Stopping for coffee and a peach scone was a breakfast routine that Callie couldn't do without. Closing her umbrella, she shook off the excess droplets and headed for the counter. Where had she gone wrong this morning? When the alarm had gone off, she had gotten up right away—well, she'd only hit Snooze twice.

The tune of "Don't Worry, Be Happy" came from her cell phone. She rifled through her bag. If only she could remember to stick her phone in that special compartment in her handbag, the one specifically for cell phones. After she removed the straw papers and gum wrappers, of course.

"Hello?"

"My pretrial hearing got cancelled, so if you want to meet for lunch today, I can do it," Heather said.

Shifting her keys to her phone hand, Callie's free fingers searched her jacket pocket for money. "I'm a community servant today, remember? I'll probably get bologna and water."

Heather laughed. "Oh, that's right. I forgot."

"Great. I'm serving time and my attorney forgot. Maybe if my attorney had been a little more—"

"I wouldn't go there if I were you. It's never a good idea to make your attorney mad."

Speaking of making her attorney mad, Callie hadn't told Heather about the new parking ticket. No point in starting her week off on the wrong foot. Besides, she'd pay this ticket on time. It was right in her handbag. Somewhere.

"Point taken. Listen, I've got to go or I'll be late. Call you tonight." While Callie stuffed her cell phone back into her handbag, her keys slipped from her fingers and crashed against the tile floor. Just as she reached down to pick them up, her hand fell upon another, much larger, stronger hand.

"Oh," she said in surprise. Straightening, she looked up, up, up, until she stared into eyes so inviting that she wanted to RSVP on the spot. "I'm so clumsy."

Tall, Dark and Handsome leaned closer, and she caught a whiff of citrus and peppermint.

"It happens to me all the time." He smiled, shifted on his leg and tucked his thumb into a belt loop on his jeans.

Something about the way this man's dark hair was combed told her nary a stray would be tolerated. He was precise. She liked that in a man.

Just beyond him she could see the rain had quieted to a soft pattering against the window-panes. The thunder murmured a romantic chant. Her insides whirled like a gentle breeze. If he lifted her on a white horse, she was *so* going with him.

"You're sure you're all right?"

The sincerity in his face and the compassion in his eyes caused her to hiccup. Her hand flew to her mouth, and she mumbled an apology.

A quirky smile lit up his face, giving him an impish look. "You'd better get some peanut butter for that."

She nodded and whipped around. Hiccupping was a family curse from her mother's side. Staccato hiccups punctuated almost every embarrassing moment. And nothing—not peanut butter or sugar or holding her breath—cured them.

He tapped her shoulder and she turned back around. "You might want these." The keys dangled between his fingers.

The brush of his hand caused her pulse to stumble. Her mind drifted to a summer's day in a park. She was wearing flowers in her hair and a long, flowing dress. He was pushing her on a swing. They were laughing together—

"What can I get you today?"

The nasally voice of the barista shook her loose from her dreaming. She wanted to thwack him. "I'll take a mocha latte and a—" she started to order her usual peach scone but quickly changed her mind "—fat-free blueberry muffin, please."

Boring, no-taste muffin in hand, Callie edged over to wait on her coffee, feeling quite proud of her self-control. Hopefully, Tall, Dark and Handsome had noticed. Unfortunately, when she turned around, her knight in shining armor was gone.

Maybe she'd exchange her muffin.

Chapter Two

Brad cranked up the engine of his old work truck. "You'd better get a grip on things, Brad, old boy, or Ryan will get his way."

Tail wagging, tongue hanging, Hammer, his yellow Lab, pranced across the seat. Brad scratched the top of the hound's head.

"She was a looker, Hammer." Brad thought about how soft her golden hair looked against the nape of her slender neck, how the lights of the coffeehouse danced in her blue eyes. Yet there was something in those baby blues—something sobering. Oh, he was reading too much into it.

"Yes, sir, she sure improved my morning." The gears groaned and squeaked as Brad shifted them into place and pulled into traffic. Too bad he hadn't gotten her number, but he'd hardly earned the privilege in that length of time. Besides, he didn't want to get serious with anyone. Though a couple of dates might have been nice.

Hammer nudged Brad's arm.

"We'll be there in a minute." Brad laughed. "It's gonna be muddy today, though. Probably not a good idea to bring you to the work site."

The dog cocked his head sideways and let out a whine. Sometimes Brad wondered if Hammer really could understand him.

"And to think I went back so I could have that strong espresso." He sighed. "If only there'd been enough time. But I can't be late for work, Hammer."

Even when it means walking away from a beautiful woman.

Flying high from her chance encounter at the bakery, Callie practically waltzed onto the job site with her coffee and muffin in hand. She didn't care that it was raining and her hair had gone flat. Let the lightning flash and the thunder rumble. The misty air rejuvenated her. In fact, she didn't even care that she was holding a fat-free muffin. She took a deep breath. Nothing like a spring rain to make her spirit soar. Absolutely nothing could ruin this day—not even the smell of lumber, which personified her dad and magnified the ache he'd left behind.

When she stepped up to the circle of people, she

noticed a man standing in the middle, his back to her, talking. A Lab sat on his haunches as though listening intently to the man. It tickled Callie to watch the dog. Maybe he was a service dog who actually helped build houses. She stifled a giggle, nibbled on her muffin and took a sip from her coffee cup. He led them into a simple prayer for the day, then dismissed them for coffee and donuts. She'd remember that tomorrow—though she didn't want to miss another opportunity of possibly running into the hunky guy at the bakery. Maybe Aunt Bonnie could tell her if he was a regular customer. On the other hand, she didn't want to encourage her aunt's matchmaking schemes.

She went to the obvious crew leader to apologize for arriving late. "I'm sorry I'm—"

The man swiveled around. His dark eyes widened and his jaw dropped.

Her pulse kicked into full throttle, and she decided right then and there this was the best day ever. Obviously, her aunt had been praying extra hard for her today. "Well, hello. Looks like we meet again." She gave her most pleasant smile to the man from the bakery.

His eyes lit up and a grin that put her heart on hold spread across his face. "Well, hello."

"Callie Easton reporting for duty." She stretched out her hand to him.

His heart-stopping grin faltered.

Maybe her aunt should try fasting next time.

He looked at his clipboard, then back at her. "*You're* Callie Easton?"

She wasn't sure whether to smile or apologize. Call her optimistic, but she could think of worse things. "That's me."

"Brad Sharp. I'm overseeing this project," he said, his words suddenly tight and professional. He probably had to be that way in front of the others. Okay, she'd play along.

She wanted to get out a pen and jot down his name, but one look in his eyes told her she would never forget it. All at once she realized her hand was still hanging out there between them, suspended, lonely and cold, while he ignored it completely.

"I see you got your coffee." His tone told her he hadn't gotten his.

Thankful she had taken the time to polish her nails, she lifted her cup and smiled. "Yes. Everyone will be happy I got it." She leaned toward him. "I'm not fun to be around if I haven't had my morning coffee. Especially on a Monday." She winked. What had gotten into her? She never winked at a man—well, not one she'd known for only less than an hour anyway. But he had rescued her keys, after all.

His gaze landed on her nails. He stared. And stared. It was as if he were in a trance.

"Coral."

Her comment visibly jarred him.

"The polish." She wiggled her fingers. "It's not a color you hear about much, you being a guy and all." *And what a guy, at that!* "You like it?"

With a blank stare he said, "Look, I don't mean to be rude, but as you can see, we serve coffee and donuts here—"

Yes, she had noticed and was ever so grateful.

"—so if you skip your trip to the bakery in the morning, you might actually make it here on time."

Her happy day paled a bit. "Is it the nail polish?" She studied her fingernails. "Admittedly not a great color for me."

He said nothing. She suddenly noticed the people around them, the number of which was growing by the second. She looked back up at him to find his gaze drilling into her.

For a moment she wondered if she should give her coffee to him. Some people had been known to snap without it. "I'll skip my trip to the bakery in the morning," Callie said. "Now if you'll excuse me." He no doubt was a busy man, and she didn't want to take up all his time. At least not yet.

"Wait. I'm not finished."

"Yes?" she asked.

"So, you'll be here by eight-thirty tomorrow morning, right?" Noticeable edge to his voice here. Okay, she had to admit his attitude was causing a teensy stir in her stomach, like a simmering pot on the stove.

"Callie?"

Why was he pressing her this way in fron of everyone? Wait. Did his foot just tap with impatience? She was pretty sure she saw that. Thoughts of her elementary-school principal, looking down at her over black-framed glasses, came back to her. She'd been in trouble that day, too.

The simmering in her stomach worked up to a full boil. It took a lot to get her riled but when she did—well, someone should warn him.

As the crowd grew, Callie's heart pounded so hard against her chest she was sure it would break through and beat this man half to death. She'd always heard there was a fine line between love and you'd-better-run.

"Right." She smiled again, but could feel it falter under the weight of her anger.

"Good." He then explained the program to her, but she didn't hear a word of it. She couldn't imagine how this rude, arrogant, man was the same suave, debonair man she'd met at the bakery.

"You need a hard hat." He pointed to her gym shoes. "And boots. Hard-toed boots."

The way he stared at her shoes made her feel

as though she had a bad pedicure. She wanted to hide her feet. "No one told me."

He blew out a sigh. A very manly, husky sigh. She ignored it. No one messed with her toes and got away with it.

"There's a pair of women's boots in my truck over there. Best put them on." He strode away without so much as a backward glance.

She couldn't believe she'd given up a perfectly tasty peach scone for this jerk. It wouldn't happen again.

"So how did your morning with the parking ticket dodger go?" Brad's sister-in-law asked as she placed a bowl of chili in front of him on the table.

"Now, Brianna, let the man alone. He's no doubt had a hard day on the job," Ryan teased.

"Yeah, like you ever leave me alone." Brad had indeed had a hard day. He hadn't meant to sound so harsh at the job site. But people were watching and if he hadn't used Callie as an example, he'd have total chaos on the job. Though they were volunteers, he still needed people to be punctual and treat the project as a real job or they'd never finish on time or produce a quality home.

Ryan shrugged and sprinkled shredded cheese over his chili. "Yeah, you're right. So how did it go?"

Across the table, their seventeen-year-old daughter, Olivia, snickered.

"Not you, too," Brad said.

"Sorry, Uncle Brad."

"Did you find a job yet, Olive?" Brad was the only one who could get by calling her that.

"Not yet. I've tried everywhere. I hope I don't get stuck babysitting the Graber twins again this year. I'm so ready for a real job."

"Nice way to change the subject, Brad," Ryan said. He turned to his daughter. "Honest work is honest work. It pays the bills. And right now you're saving for college. Which reminds me, did you go to the library and check on those scholarship options yet?"

"Dad, can we talk about this later?"

"We can and we will," Ryan said in an unmistakably firm tone.

Olivia turned to Brad and smiled. "So, tell us about your day."

"I'll get you later," he hissed at his grinning niece.

Brad explained how he'd run into Callie at the bakery and how she'd turned up late at the job site. When he finished, everyone was quiet. He could feel Ryan studying him.

"What?" Brad tried to appear nonchalant.

Ryan exchanged a glance with Brianna, then

turned twinkling eyes to Brad. Judges' eyes weren't supposed to twinkle.

"Nothing." Ryan looked at Brianna once again. "Did I say anything?"

"I didn't hear anything," she said.

He turned back to Brad. "Nothing here."

"Look, Ryan, I've told you. I'm not interested in a relationship. I'm waiting for my next missionary assignment in South America. I'm only here because of Mom."

"I don't know why when there's plenty to do here," Ryan said.

"I don't question why you want to be a judge."

"You're not getting any younger," Ryan said.

Brad took a bite of the spicy chili in front of him. It was fiery hot but he didn't let on.

There was no denying that Callie Easton was eye candy, but he'd seen her type before. He couldn't deal with the nail polish, the hair, the makeup,....

"She primps, plucks and pedicures, Ryan."

"They all do that."

"Remember, Nicole started out that way, obsessing over her appearance. One thing led to another until—"

"You can't compare every woman who dabs on nail polish to our sister. She had issues. She was sick, Brad."

"I don't want to talk about it."

"Okay, matter dropped," Ryan said, followed by a moment of silence.

Brad knew he had been hard on Callie, but he didn't want her around the job site. She was a distraction, and he figured she liked it that way. The sooner they could get through this job, the better.

"You know, little brother, you could use a haircut."

He goes from one complaint about me to another. Brad's hand rubbed the back of his neck. "It's not that bad. But my barber retired, so I'll have to find someone soon." Brad swirled the chili around in his bowl.

"I go to that place behind the bakery you said you visited this morning. It's called the Peaches & Cream Salon. As far as I'm concerned, it's the best place in town. You ought to check it out," Brianna said.

Brad turned to Ryan. "Do you go there?"

He shook his head. "I go to a shop near the courthouse. But that's out of your way."

Brad thought a moment and nodded. "Maybe I'll do that." Thankful to talk about anything but his love life, Brad made a mental note to check out the salon.

Callie looked at her client's cranberry-polished nails. "That's it, Mrs. Frantz. You're free to go."

"Thank you, dear." The old woman stuffed a ten-dollar tip into Callie's hand, then hobbled out the door.

"What is she, three hundred years old by now?" Jessica asked, opening a box and examining the contents.

"Jessica, shh—she will hear you."

"Her?" Jessica asked, pointing. "That woman hasn't heard anything since 1973. She's got pretty nails, though, I'll give her that."

Callie suppressed a giggle and began to clean her manicure station. "You'd better behave yourself or Aunt Bonnie will get you."

"Yeah, right. I've seen puppies more fierce than her on her worst day."

Everyone knew Aunt Bonnie was as sweet as they came.

Jessica glanced at her watch. "You sure you can cover for me while I take Mom to the doctor?"

"Absolutely. You go ahead and go." Callie looked at the box of new inventory. "Hey, didn't we get another box of the setting gel?"

"Yeah, a small one. It's in the back room," Jessica said, without looking up.

"Great. Let me get that before you take off."

"No problem."

As Callie walked into the back room, she heard the front door swoosh open. A man's voice said someone had recommended he come to the salon for a haircut.

"It just so happens there's a stylist in the back who can help you. Go ahead and take a seat by the wash basin." Jessica popped into the back room. "You have a customer." She raised her eyebrows and let out a low whistle. "Too bad I have to leave."

Callie rolled her eyes and walked past her toward the front. Facing the back of the customer's head, Callie pulled product from the shelf.

"So, this is your first time here?" she asked, working the shampoo into his hair.

"Uh-huh." His words vibrated as her fingers massaged his scalp.

He didn't offer anything else, so Callie let her mind meander while she finished the job. Once she rinsed away the bubbles, she flipped up his chair and towel-dried his hair.

"If you'll follow me," she said, leading the way to her cutting station.

He settled into his seat. She swiveled him around to face the mirror. That's when they saw each other for the first time. Callie's tongue stuck to the roof of her mouth. By the look of Brad Sharp, she would say he wasn't doing any better.

"I, uh, my sister-in-law told me to come here.

I didn't know you worked here. My barber retired, I needed a place—"

The way his words tumbled into one another might have been funny if she wasn't still mad at him for his behavior on the job.

She swung the scissors toward him, opening and closing them a couple of times for good measure. He squirmed in his seat, which satisfied her immensely.

"My aunt and uncle own this place. This is where I work." Snip, snip, snip. He had nice hair. Really didn't need much of a cut, but guys like him kept their hair groomed to perfection.

"Listen, about this morning—"

"Yes?" She stopped and stared at him through the mirror. She kept the scissors poised and dangerously close to his ear. Clint Eastwood's words played in her head. *Go ahead, make my day."

"I'm sorry if I came across too harsh."

Well, she hadn't seen that one coming. Snip, snip, snip. "Don't worry about it. You did what you had to do."

She could feel him looking at her and glanced at him through the mirror.

"Thanks." It was all he said, but the way he said it sent a slow tingle that started at the top of her spine and shimmied all the way down.

"So how did you get into construction?" she

asked, warmth spreading through her fingers as they brushed the back of his neck and feathered through his hair.

"I've been at it for as long as I can remember. I've worked overseas, building homes for the poor."

She stopped cutting and looked up at him. "Really?" Her toppled knight in shining armor was quickly regaining his position on the white horse.

They discussed the Make a Home project when suddenly a telephone call on his cell phone cut their conversation short. Thankfully, she had finished his hair before he had to go. He paid for his trim and bounded out of the salon as quickly as his legs could carry him.

She couldn't help wondering what had really brought him to their salon.

Chapter Three

Brianna and Ryan were in this together. Someone was going to pay.

Brad peeled out of the parking lot faster than he had intended. The last thing he wanted was for Callie to witness his little outburst. He was thankful a caller with a wrong number gave him an excuse to leave.

"I don't believe she did this to me." One glance at the speedometer told him he'd better settle down or *he'd* be standing before the judge. At the first stoplight, he picked up his cell phone and hit speed dial.

"Hello?" Ryan said with disgusting innocence.

"You set me up," Brad snapped.

"What are you talking about?"

"Come on, Ryan, you know good and well what I'm talking about. Brianna purposely sent me to that hair place because Callie Easton works there."

"She does?"

"Oh, no, you don't. You of all people should know lying doesn't work."

"Okay, so we knew she worked there. What's the big deal? It's still a great place for a haircut. You needed a recommendation, and Brianna gave you one. What's the harm?"

A growl rumbled in his throat.

"Listen, little brother, I'd like to talk with you, but Brianna's just put dinner on the table. You know how she is when dinner gets cold. Talk to you later."

"Oh, that's nice. Real nice." Brad tossed his phone on the seat and sped off. His gut coiled. The last thing he wanted was for Callie to think he was interested. Okay, so he'd flirted with her at the bakery. But knowing she was a plant of his brother's changed things and the princess image didn't sit well with him, either. No matter how much her blue eyes sparkled in the sunlight, and her soft hands felt warm against his skin.

Once home, Brad stepped into his office. He handled all his paperwork for his jobs from his office at home, saving him the expense of a secretary. Keeping expenses down and doing some extra carpentry work on the side afforded him the opportunity to oversee the Make a Home projects and save money to go back to work in South America. He may not be rich, but he enjoyed his life—as a bachelor.

He went out now and then, but he hadn't met anyone he would want to share his life with. In fact, he'd given up on the idea. He could think of worse things than bachelorhood. Besides, he'd been too busy to think about women lately.

Hammer trotted into the room and gave Brad's leg a nudge. He reached down and rubbed his back. "How you doing, boy?"

Sticking two invoices into their appropriate files, Brad sharpened a couple of pencils, stuck them in his caddy and took a final glance around the room. Satisfied that everything was in its place, he walked out.

"Come on, boy," he called to Hammer, closing the door behind them. "Let's go see Mom."

Ryan could push all he wanted. Brad was standing firm. He had a good life, and he didn't need a woman—especially a woman with painted nails and a punctuality problem. "I've seen plenty of pretty women in my day. She is just one more."

End of story.

Callie couldn't make sense out of Brad's visit to the salon. Did he really just want a haircut?

She'd like to think he came there on purpose, but he was obviously surprised to see her. Was that an act? Was he checking up on her? Working undercover? If so, why? She disregarded a couple of parking tickets, for crying out loud. Was that a crime? Well, maybe it was a crime, but it wasn't exactly a felony.

She pulled her car into her aunt and uncle's driveway. She could use some distraction from thinking about Brad Sharp.

"Come on in, honey," Aunt Bonnie said as she opened the front door.

The spicy scent of herbed pork chops and buttery potatoes filled the air. Callie followed her nose to the kitchen.

"Smells awesome," she said.

Dressed in jeans, a pink flowing blouse and a full-length apron, Aunt Bonnie was leaning over, peering into the oven. "Looks good." She closed the oven door, then walked over and gave Callie a hug. "Oh, you're getting skinnier."

That's why she loved her aunt.

"So, how was your day?"

"Why—why do you ask?" Callie stammered.

With a confused expression, Bonnie pulled off her oven mitts. "Well, I didn't have much chance to talk to you at the salon, and I was just wondering how your community service has been going."

Callie hated to be suspicious, but sometimes Aunt Bonnie was innocence, sometimes snoop queen. Right now, Callie wasn't sure which.

"It was fine, really. Building a house is pretty amazing. I had no idea how much went into it." Callie grabbed some glasses and filled them with ice and water, attempting to forget the humiliation of yesterday morning, the look on Brad's face, his biting words. At least she'd made it on time this morning.

"Any handsome young men working there?" Aunt Bonnie's eyes twinkled with mischief.

"Why, are you in the market?"

Aunt Bonnie giggled. "Oh, you," she said.

"Uncle George home yet?" Callie placed the glasses on the table.

"No, but he should be home any second." Bonnie gathered serving spoons. "Are you trying to change the subject?"

Just then they heard the garage door open and Uncle George's car creeping into his parking spot. Not that it was hard to do. He kept an immaculate garage. Callie wished his organizational skills had rubbed off on her.

"There are my girls." Uncle George hung his keys on a wooden peg by the door, walked over and kissed Aunt Bonnie soundly on the lips, then gave Callie a peck on the cheek. "How's your community service going? Any eligible bachelors?"

Callie sighed.

Uncle George laughed and shrugged. "Just wondered."

They were hopeless romantics, no doubt about it.

Callie slid into her chair and placed her napkin on her lap. "If you must know, it was fine." They stared at her. "And, um, no reason to get your hopes up."

Their shoulders slumped in unison.

Uncle George said grace over their meal, scooped out a dollop of mashed potatoes, then passed the bowl to Callie.

"You got your new work crew lined up for the ice-cream shop, Uncle George?"

"I'm working on it. I still have one more position to fill, and I'm not real happy with the applications I have left. It's hard to find good help these days."

Callie suddenly imagined Brad saying the same thing.

Once dinner was over, Callie and Aunt Bonnie cleaned the table and washed the dishes while Uncle George went into the living room and relaxed in front of the television. He was as sweet as they came, but when it came to kitchen duties, he was fully convinced they were a woman's job.

Aunt Bonnie said he made up for it by helping with the laundry.

Callie wanted a man who wasn't afraid to do both. An image of Brad in an apron popped into her head. Yeah, that would be the day.

"What are you thinking about?" Aunt Bonnie asked while maneuvering a long pan into the cupboard.

"Nothing much." Callie worked her fingers through the soap bubbles for more silverware.

"I don't know why we just didn't load the dishwasher," Aunt Bonnie said.

Callie shrugged. "I thought it might soften my hands after working construction for two days."

Her aunt laughed.

"Aunt Bonnie, do you think Dad ever thinks of me?"

The older woman closed the cupboard door and walked over to Callie. "I'm sure he does, every single day, honey." Bonnie reached up and stroked Callie's cheek, her soft hand protective and maternal. "I've no doubt he would love to see you, but he's waited so long that now he probably wouldn't know how to do it."

Callie dried her hands and sat down at the clean table. "I wish I knew how to contact him."

With her warm brown eyes fixed on Callie, Bonnie sat across from her and patted her hand.

"I know, Cal," she said softly. "Something stirring up thoughts of your dad lately?"

"Oh, working at the house, smelling the lumber, hearing the pounding hammers, all that, I guess."

A pensive look in her eyes, Aunt Bonnie hesitated a moment and nodded. "I can see how that would make you think of him." A pause hovered between them.

"No one stays around," Callie said, slumping further into her chair. "Except you and Uncle George, of course."

Aunt Bonnie smiled. "There is One who never leaves."

"I know." Callie didn't want to get into another deep talk about God. She knew the scriptures and all that "He'll never leave you or forsake you" stuff. She wanted to believe it, but doubts plagued her. Her dad had left, her fiancé, Jeremy, had left—what was to stop God?

Bonnie grabbed Callie's hand. "Look, I know things have been a little dry for you lately. Talk to Him." With that, Aunt Bonnie released Callie's hand, gave it a pat and went back over to the oven. "You know, when you were a kid, you used to help your dad around the house."

Callie perked up. She always loved to hear stories about her family.

"Until one day, you pounded a little too hard when hanging a nail for a picture and there was no stud. Your hammer went clear through the drywall."

Callie winced. "I haven't improved in my home-building skills all that much."

Aunt Bonnie chuckled. "Well, community service will be over soon enough."

Callie didn't know what to think about that. Part of her wanted to run from it because it reminded her of her father, and another part of her wanted to run to it, because the memories were all she had left.

If only people she loved wouldn't leave.

"Hey, Mom." Brad stepped into his childhood home, the stale odor of a house closed up assaulting him. He thought his staying in town for a while would help her, but she was sinking deeper into despair.

"Hi, Brad." Annie Sharp pushed herself to a sitting position on the sofa, propped the pillow behind her and worked her fingers through shoulder-length brown tangles.

In her late fifties, his mom still didn't have a smidgen of gray. With her big dark eyes and trademark thick locks, men once sought after his mother. But these days she looked too thin, and even he could tell her hair needed professional help. No doubt the same could be said of her inner self.

Brad walked over and pulled open the living-room curtains. Late afternoon sunlight chased away the gloom. He could see Hammer waiting patiently in the truck.

"Aw, Brad, why did you do that?" She shielded her eyes. "That gives me a headache."

"Mom, you need to let some sunshine in. It's a beautiful day out there."

She rubbed her eyes and yawned. "What time is it?"

"It's five. Have you started dinner—more important, have you had lunch?"

"Now, Brad, don't you start."

He sagged into the cushion beside her and took her limp hands into his. "Mom, you have to take care of yourself."

With her eyes cast down, she whispered, "I know."

"Are you taking your vitamins?"

She shrugged.

"Let me take you out to dinner."

She glanced up. "Oh, no, no, Brad. I'm a mess." She absently ran a hand over her hair again.

"So go get cleaned up." He wondered how long she'd been in those wrinkled clothes.

"Thank you, honey, but I'm too tired to go anywhere."

"Mom. When was the last time you left this

house?" Stray wrappers, newspapers, paper plates and empty glasses littered the room. Guilt speared him. He needed to make sure she got out once in a while. He should have been coming over more often. Work had gotten in the way of his good judgment—again.

She shrugged.

"You need to get out."

"I will. I have to go to the nursing home soon and see your grandmother."

She leaned back against the sofa as though she barely had the strength to talk.

"How's Gram doing?" He hadn't been over there in a while, either.

"'Bout the same. She misses Princess." Princess was a nickname Nicole had been given as a small child. To Brad, the name had been prophetic. She had fallen into what he called the "princess curse," where women think they have to have the perfect bodies, yet in their minds their bodies are never good enough. That curse had killed his sister, and left a huge hole in their family.

"We all miss her. But Nicole would want us to go on, Mom." He told himself that every day.

She lifted dark, watery eyes. "I try. I really do." Tears slipped down her cheeks.

"I know." He pulled her frail body to him. "Let me take you to see Gram tomorrow."

She finally pulled away, teetering a moment, then dabbed her nose with a tissue. "You have a job to do."

"Well, how about I pick up dinner and then take you to see Gram, after I get off work?"

"I don't know."

He looked at her tattered clumps of hair. "I could even take you out to get your hair done, to make you feel better."

For a moment he thought he saw a flicker of excitement. But she said, "I'm not ready for that, Brad."

Disappointment flooded him. What could he do to help his mom? Right now she looked so…old. Lifeless.

"But if you'll take me to see your grandma in the next day or two, that would be good."

He'd take what he could get. "Great. In the meantime, I'm running to that Chinese restaurant down the road that you love. I'll pick you up some dinner. Be right back."

As though she were too weary to argue, she leaned back into her pillow. "Okay, honey."

He suspected she would drift back to sleep before he pulled out of the driveway.

"How you doing this morning?" Heather's hyper voice said she'd already downed two cups of coffee. Callie could hear the whir of her car engine and the swishing of traffic in the background.

"It's just so wrong that you're this happy in the morning. Please don't tell me you're already on your way to work." Callie settled onto the foot of her soft bed blanketed with billowy comforters. Chaos, her sandy-haired cocker spaniel puppy, trotted over to her and tried to get on the bed. With the mounds of blankets, it was too hard for him to jump up. Callie snatched her pooch and snuggled into his silky fur.

"Okay, I won't tell you."

Callie giggled when Chaos tried to lick her face. "Stop."

"Are you listening to me or playing with that dog again?"

"Guilty on both counts."

Heather sighed. "Tossed aside for a puppy."

"You're not as cute."

"Can't argue with you there."

"So, why are you off and running this morning?" Callie asked.

"I've got an early hearing."

"Well, I'm in no hurry to do my community service, but you'll be happy to know I'm making an effort to get there on time."

"That a girl."

"They'd better save me some coffee, that's all I've got to say."

"Well, behave yourself. I don't have time to represent you on any criminal charges just now."

"Thanks for the heads-up. I'll certainly keep that in mind before I go out and commit my next crime." Tucking himself into a perfect circle, Chaos settled onto her lap.

Heather laughed. "So how do you like working with Brad Sharp?"

"Wow, I'm impressed that you remembered his name."

"Oh, uh, well—"

"Hey, wasn't that the judge's last name? Sharp?"

"Uh, yes—yes, I think it was." Heather was stuttering. Heather never stuttered.

"I smell a rat."

"What are you talking about?"

"Is he related to Judge Sharp?"

"Well, it is entirely possible. They both have the same last name, after all."

"Wouldn't that be a conflict of interest or something?" This whole matter did not sit right with her. Something was going on.

"Just because he's having you do community service on a project with his brother does not merit a conflict of interest."

"Aha, so you admit it!" Callie was incensed.

"Well, yeah, I do. So Brad is his brother. What's the big deal?"

"Just seems like they're in cahoots about something. And actually it seems like you might be involved, Heather. Do you know Brad?"

"What? I can't hear you, Callie. You're breaking up," Heather said.

"Did you have something to do with—"

"Listen, I'm at the office, and I can't hear you anyway. Gotta go! Talk to you later."

Callie had a sneaking suspicion that Heather could hear her just fine. She donned her boot-cut jeans and a royal-blue-and-white-striped T-shirt. Once her hair was dried to satisfaction, she put Chaos in his crate, then grabbed her straw bag with blue matching trim before heading out the door.

Something strange was going on, and Callie was determined to find out what it was—even if it meant talking to a man who probably wanted nothing to do with her.

Brad watched Callie give the board one final thump with the hammer, and then admire her handiwork. Just then, she glanced over at Brad, making him drop the box of nails he was holding, scattering them across the concrete floor.

They both fell on their knees and started gathering the runaway nails before someone tripped on them.

"Over here," she said, laughing.

All around them, people crawled around the floor in search of the nails. In a rippling effect, one-by-one, people started laughing, until the entire crew was nearly hysterical.

Brad quickly stood, blew out a ragged breath and put his silent cell phone to his ear. Clomping his way through the rough terrain, he moved away from the job site. He needed a minute to think, to try and figure out what had gotten into him.

He kicked a clump of dirt out of the way. He was an idiot, and a clumsy one at that. Hammer stepped away, walked behind him and ended up on his other side.

Brad had tried to avoid her. He wanted nothing to do with her, thanks to his brother. Yet when he noticed how hard she was working, sunlight glistening in her golden hair, cheeks flushed, tongue peeking out of the side of her determined mouth with every measured swing, well, he tried to look away, but he couldn't.

"Hey, are you all right?" The soft touch of Callie's hand on his arm made him whip around as though she were an enemy to be reckoned with.

"I'm fine." He glared at Hammer for not letting him know someone was approaching.

"Didn't mean to startle you. I just wanted to apologize. I wasn't, um, laughing at you. It was just a funny situation."

A sliver of vulnerability shone in her eyes, pulling him in. The slight sprinkle of freckles across her nose gave her a childlike quality, though he knew from experience she had no trouble standing up for herself. Not that that was bad. She was the perfect blend of independence and softness. He liked that in a woman.

"Brad?" She stepped closer. "Are you all right?" She touched him again, sending electrical impulses shooting straight up his arm. Her eyes probed his, lingering, searching.

Ammunition straight from his brother's warehouse.

Oh, she was good, no doubt about it. He took a step backward. "I'm fine." Sweat beaded on his forehead. He took another step backward. "Really." Dropping his cell phone, he bent over and picked it up, shaking his head at another display of clumsiness.

"You're not mad at me, then?" The question in her eyes, the lift of her mouth, the way her slender finger curled around a strand of hair…

Taking another step backward, his foot fell into a hole, and he went down with a thud. Much to his embarrassment, a groan escaped him.

"Oh, let me help you," she said, reaching over to help him up.

"No, no, don't move me." His voice sounded three octaves too high. He cleared his throat and said with a deep, manly voice, "I've hurt my ankle."

This woman was dangerous. He'd stay away from her or die trying.

"I'll get some help." Before he could respond, she was off and running. And the weird thing was his dog, who never left his side, went with her.

The traitor.

By the looks of his ankle, running was something he wouldn't be doing anytime soon.

His brother was going to live to rue the day Callie Easton stepped into his courthouse.

Chapter Four

"Come on, Brad, it's only a sprain. You'll be on crutches for two, three days. What's the big deal?" Ryan said.

Rain pelted the windows of Brad's house, interrupting Hammer's slumber. The Lab scratched behind his ear, then sauntered into the kitchen, leaving Brad stranded in the living room.

"The big deal? The big deal?" The words wrapped around his esophagus and threatened his air supply. Brad took a long, ragged breath and propped his leg on a pillow while reclining on the sofa. "The big deal is I am trying to build a house."

"A couple of days on crutches won't kill you." The phone wire crackled with the thunderstorm, matching Brad's mood.

A low, throbbing pain started at the back of his

head and radiated forward. "Listen, I've got to go. My head aches and I need something to eat."

"You want Brianna to bring you over something?"

You've done enough already, thank you. "No. I'll just grab something."

"You need to learn to cook. There are times when you might not be able to get to the restaurant."

Just once he'd like Ryan to take off his big brother hat.

"I've said it before, and I'll say it again. You will never find me in the kitchen. I have an aversion to working in a kitchen. Call me a male chauvinist, but it's not my thing."

"You might not want to mention that on first dates." Ryan laughed.

"Talk to you later." Brad hung up the phone, feeling grumpier than ever. He reached for the pain pills the hospital had given him and took two. His stomach growled. Hammer's paws clacked against the hardwood. With his plastic food bowl clutched between his teeth, Hammer stopped at the sofa in front of Brad. Then he dropped it.

"This is your second fill-up today. I've yet to eat anything."

Hammer plunked down on his haunches, lifted sad eyes and commenced with a soulful whine.

"You know, that little act could make you a Hollywood star." Brad snatched the bowl and his crutches and stood up. "You owe me." He was headed toward the kitchen when the doorbell rang.

If his mood got any worse, he'd have to hole himself up in a padded cell, he thought, hobbling to the door. "If you're not a Girl Scout selling cookies, go away." The hinges creaked as the door swung open.

There stood Callie Easton under a red-and-white polka-dotted umbrella big enough to cover a baseball team. It all but screamed to his nosy neighbors to sit up and take notice. She stood there smiling.

Couldn't she think of anything better to do?

"Whoa, looks like I came in the nick of time," she said, smiling brightly.

Brad continued to stare at her. It irritated him to no end that someone could be that happy all the time. Okay, his mood was so bad he didn't even want to be around himself.

"Color me biased," she said, pointing at the dog food bowl, "but I think you'll prefer this." She nodded toward her own dish.

He forced a weak laugh. They stood there in awkward silence.

"Um, it's kind of wet out here. Mind if I come in?"

Cold chills swept over him. The smell of danger was in the air. Or maybe it was the smell of fear. His.

"Yeah, sure. Come on in." Though he thought better of it, he stepped away from the door so she could slip inside.

"I felt so bad about what happened at work. And I couldn't help wondering if I caused it somehow. All those nails rolling everywhere, me laughing, the others joining in—"

Yeah, thanks for bringing it all up again.

"—so where's your kitchen?"

"This way." He adjusted his crutches and walked ahead of her. "You didn't need—"

"Cooking is something I enjoy doing now and then, when I have the time." She started to place the hot dish on the counter then turned to him. "You have a towel you can put here so the heat doesn't hurt your counter?" She looked down. "Oh, hi, Hammer."

The dog trotted over to her as though they were the best of friends. *No more treats for that Benedict Arnold. Generic dog food. Starting tomorrow.*

"Yeah, let me get it." He hobbled over to the drawer, pulled out a towel and laid it down haphazardly.

Callie put the casserole dish on top. "Hope you like lasagna." Before he could respond, she said,

"I have breadsticks and salad in the car. I'll be right back."

What was she up to? He watched her head out the door. She was dressed to kill, and he was afraid he just might be the victim. He'd better be careful. She could be in on this plan with his brother.

While she was outside, he hobbled as fast as he could to the bathroom to check his hair. He ran a quick comb through it, then went back out to meet her. There was no law that said he couldn't look nice.

"Oh, there you are. I wondered where you'd disappeared to." She placed the other food on the counter.

He noticed she was barefoot. Her perfectly manicured red toenails made him stiffen. Princess.

She caught him looking. "I didn't want to mess up your floor with my dirty shoes."

The sincerity in her voice softened him. His brother had made him paranoid with his sneaky matchups, and Brad found it hard to relax where Ryan was concerned. But looking at Callie just now, he couldn't imagine Ryan had anything to do with this.

He took a deep breath. "This is really nice, Callie. But there's way too much food here."

She shrugged. "Don't you believe in leftovers?"

"No, I never have leftovers."

She blinked.

"I never cook. Always go out to eat, so there aren't leftovers." He started to say something about kitchen work not being his forte, but he remembered his brother's words and kept his mouth shut.

Which was stupid, really, considering he had no intention of having a relationship with this woman.

"Always eat out?" She looked around his kitchen, and he wondered if he should apologize. For what, he didn't know.

"Nothing wrong with that. There's only me. And I like to eat out." His words sounded gruff, but he was okay with that.

"Oh, I understand perfectly," she said with irritating amusement in her voice. "You don't have to explain to me."

"I wasn't explaining to you, I was merely—" His jaw twitched. Why did he get defensive around her? She was a nice woman and he acted like a jerk when she was around. The throbbing in his ankle now matched the pounding in his head. He blamed his attitude on that.

She held up her hand. "I didn't come here to fight." She glanced at his ankle. "Besides, I'd just have to trip you and I'd win." She laughed.

The pain in his ankle increased tenfold.

"Let's start again. I came here to give you dinner." She pointed at his foot. "I hear you sprained it."

"Yeah."

"I'm glad it's not broken."

He took a deep breath, trying to keep his aggravation to himself. The medication kicked in and his eyelids drooped.

"Well, I'd better go. Just wanted to drop that off," she said cheerfully. Callie started to walk past him and he grabbed her arm. Her soft, slender, warm-to-the-touch arm. "Don't go," he whispered.

Surprise flared in her eyes.

"There's so much food here. Stay and have dinner with me." He heard himself say it but couldn't believe the words had jumped out of his own mouth. The meds brought back the niceness in him. He knew it had to be deep down in there somewhere.

She hesitated.

"Please?" *What is the matter with me? Run, hide, before it's too late!*

"Okay."

They stood there a moment looking at each other, and adrenaline shot through him. He would not fall for this woman. But there was no law that said he couldn't enjoy her company.

Just this once.

It was all Callie could do not to laugh at the way Brad maneuvered around the kitchen. She wasn't the cruel sort, but it was obvious this man wasn't used to physical pain or inconvenience.

"That was a great meal, really, Callie. Thank you." Brad settled onto the sofa beside her.

"You're welcome." Her fingers worked through the back of her hair. She hoped it wasn't too flat from the rain.

"Where did you learn to cook like that?"

She shrugged. "Aunt Bonnie doesn't enjoy cooking, and she's always been too busy running the Peaches & Cream businesses to spend much time in the kitchen. So, wanting to help her out, I sort of picked it up myself. Watching the cooking channels helps."

"Well, I'm impressed. As I said, I avoid the kitchen."

"It's always good to challenge yourself, you know."

"Oh, are you the expert now?" he teased.

"Well, I am building a house, after all." She straightened in her seat and took a contented breath.

"You think you could take over for me tomorrow so I could let my ankle heal?"

She whipped her head around to him and he laughed.

"For a minute there, I thought you were serious."

He leaned in toward her and whispered, "I was serious." He winked.

His breath brushed against her cheek. Chill bumps climbed her arms. She wanted to move but couldn't so much as breathe. Brad looked deeply into her eyes, then traveled down to her mouth as his head tilted forward, leaning closer, closer. She couldn't believe this was happening, not after the way he'd treated her on the site. Did Brad Sharp actually…like her? Like the slight touch of a breeze, his lips barely lit upon hers. And she let out a hiccup that shook the sofa.

Her eyes flew open. Brad blinked and pulled away.

It was a curse. *Thanks, Mom.*

Callie mentally shook herself. What was she thinking? By the look on Brad's face, she'd say the situation had caught him by surprise, as well. Or maybe it was just the hiccup.

"It's getting late. I'd better be going. Just bring my dishes to the work site whenever you're finished with them." Practically sprinting to the door, she turned with a wave before he could haul himself off the sofa. "Hope you feel better." Hiccups punctuated the night air as she scurried to her car.

Once inside, Callie tried to catch her breath and straighten out her thinking. She wasn't sure why she'd decided that bringing Brad dinner was a good idea. Maybe because she felt bad about his ankle, or because she wanted to find out if he, too, thought it was suspicious that she'd been sent to his job site and he'd been sent to her salon. But it certainly hadn't occurred to her that they'd end up almost kissing on his couch.

It was probably just the painkillers, that's all. Well, that would explain *his* behavior—but it wouldn't explain the fact that her heart was still pounding from the feel of his lips on hers.

Hiccup.

Brad put his palm against his forehead and leaned his head against the back of the sofa. His mind was cloudy from the meds, but he was alert enough to know he had just tried to kiss Callie Easton. What was the matter with him? Number one, he refused to get entangled with a woman his brother had forced on him, and number two, he'd only known her for a few days. Not only that, but he wasn't staying in Burrow forever. So what was the point of a relationship here? He had to blame it on the meds. He just didn't work that fast under normal circumstances. Now she probably thought he was a real player.

"I blew it again," he said, feeling Hammer's head pushing against his hand. "A lot of help you are. I know you're the friendly sort, but where's your allegiance, huh?" Brad scratched behind his pooch's ears. "You need to keep me away from her, not make her your new best friend."

He'd have to watch himself in the days ahead and stay away from Callie at all costs. Keep their relationship on a purely professional level. A few weeks and it would all be over…until his brother sent over someone else. Though something told him someone else wouldn't have the same power over him as Callie Easton.

The smell of sweet apple conditioner filled the air. Callie tried to relax while Jessica ran the warm water over her hair. "I will *so* pay you back for this, Jessica. I promise."

"Don't worry about it. I told you I have nothing to do tonight anyway. Besides, I didn't have that many appointments this afternoon."

"I will name my firstborn after you. I've always liked the name Jessica, so that will work just fine, don't you think?"

Jessica laughed. "That will be the day." Jessica worked the conditioner through Callie's hair.

"Hey, what do you mean by that?"

"Only that your aunt has been trying to hook you up for years."

Why did people constantly pressure her to find someone? Marriage wasn't for everybody. If she was happy with her life as it was, why couldn't they leave her alone?

"Is the water too hot?" Jessica asked.

"No, it's perfect."

"I've waited all through the color and highlights, so now you want to tell me what's going on?"

"What are you talking about?"

"Come on, Callie. We both know you only color your hair when you're really, really upset. You have issues, girlfriend."

"Thank you, Dr. Phil."

"Now spill it."

Callie sighed. "Brad sprained his ankle because of me, so I brought him dinner as a peace offering. And he almost…kissed me."

"Do you like him?" Jessica turned off the water and rubbed Callie's hair with a towel.

"I'm confused. I thought *he* didn't like *me*. But I guess he's a friend."

"Is that all?"

"Yes." Callie pushed the lever to lower the bottom half of her reclining chair.

"Is that all you want him to be?" Jessica led the way to her station.

"Ye-yes."

"Are you sure?"

Callie slid into the chair. "Jessica?"

"Yes?"

"Could you stop asking me these questions?"

Jessica laughed. "Suit yourself."

Callie steered the conversation to safe waters during her trim. Jessica didn't push, for which Callie was thankful.

"I love it, Jess." Callie swirled around in her chair and looked at the back through a handheld mirror. "I haven't had light brown hair in forever." She wondered if Brad would like it, then wondered if she should be wondering that.

"It's really a good look for you, Cal." Jessica glanced at the clock. "Well, now I really do need to get home. My favorite show is coming on in fifteen minutes." Jessica finished sweeping the hair from her station.

Callie gave her a hug and sneaked a twenty into Jessica's purse when she wasn't looking. "See you tomorrow."

"Let me know what he thinks of it," Jessica called out.

"Who?"

Jessica just smiled. "Good night, Callie."

Brad glanced at his watch. Callie had been so careful to be on time at the site since that first day. After last night things would no doubt be a little awkward between them. He was an idiot. He had no intention of getting involved with this woman—

or anyone else, for that matter, and yet he did something stupid like that. What if she didn't show up again? He'd have to tell his brother the truth so that she didn't get in trouble. Brad shifted on his crutches. That was all he needed.

If she didn't show up in the next ten minutes, he'd call her and tell her that despite what happened last night, she was still expected to show up for duty.

A car pulled up in front of the job site, and the Sauders family piled out.

"Good morning, Brad," Mick said, stepping up to the house.

"Morning, Mick and Andrea." Brad looked at Micah. "How come you're not in school?" He ruffled her blonde curls, and she lifted the snaggletoothed grin of an eight-year-old.

"We're headed there now. Thought we'd stop by and see how things were coming first," Mick said.

Brad walked the family through the framing, showing the progress they were making, pointing out where each room will be and introducing some of the volunteers. Brad walked over to a woman whose back was to them. He didn't recognize her. "And this is—" He waited for her to turn around, but she didn't. She just kept hammering. He looked at the Sauders and they smiled.

Micah walked up to the woman and tapped her on the arm.

She turned around. Three nails were gripped between her lips. She pulled them free, then yanked the earbuds from her ears, music spilling from them. "Oh, hello," she said.

Brad was speechless—again. It was Callie, with someone else's hair.

She tossed a brief glance at Brad, then quickly looked back toward the family.

"Uh, Callie Easton, this is the Sauders family. They will be moving into this home."

Callie took in a sharp breath. "Oh my, it's so nice to meet you!" She pumped their hands with great enthusiasm. "It's so fun to put the faces with the work—you know what I mean?"

They stared at her, blankly.

"You know, you work and work and have no idea who you're doing it for or if they'll like it or if they'll want to move first chance they get. You wonder what kind of family they are, you know, the lively type or the—"

Brad turned toward the Sauders. "I know you have to get to work, so we'll let you go." He edged them toward the door.

Micah walked over to Callie and tapped her leg. Callie looked down. "Yes?"

"I like you." With that, Micah walked back over to her parents.

"I like you, too," Callie called out happily to the little girl before sticking the earbuds back into her ears.

Once Brad said his goodbyes to the family, he turned back to the work at hand. His crew worked busily, hammering away. He had to admit that Callie was a real trooper. She hammered with the best of them and kept up a steady pace. Brad sneaked a look from time to time, to see how she was doing.

He looked at her once more and scratched his head. Somewhere between dinner and breakfast, she had managed to change her entire look.

Why would she do that?

Chapter Five

After lunch the rain that had started in the late morning had evaporated and the team was called in to work on the roofing. Men talking, boots scraping against plywood, the lingering smell of spring rains. It surprised Callie how much she enjoyed those smells and sounds. They brought a certain comfort she couldn't explain. Sometimes she thought she could turn around and find her dad there, watching her work.

"Hey, Callie," one of the workers said. "Brad had to run to the hardware store. We're working on the roof. If you want to grab that staple gun, you can join us. We're running behind." He climbed the ladder to the roof.

Callie swallowed hard and swallowed hard again. And then one more time for good measure. *He wants me to go up on the roof. Me. Callie*

Easton—who won't even climb a stepladder—on the roof.

Okay, no problem. She could do this. She wasn't a wimp. If those guys could do it, so could she. Willing air back into her lungs, she walked over, grabbed the staple gun and climbed the ladder that loomed before her.

Though she was no fashion statement, she was thankful for her sturdy boots. When she made it on the roof, she dared to take another breath. A big one. It might have to last her awhile.

After someone explained the job to her, she ignored the threatening nausea, kept her gaze fixed on the roof and refused to look down. She began to staple the felt underlay onto the plywood, making sure she overlapped each course to the one before it. After some time she relaxed a little, though she was careful to hold herself steady. Her hand gripped the staple gun as she moved it along the felt.

What would her dad think if he could see her now? Did he ever think of her? Did he wish he could see her again? Maybe he had a new family and barely remembered her at all. If only her mom hadn't—

The spring winds whipped up the edge of the underlay, and she steadied it, being careful not to move too much. The sweet scent of honeysuckle lifted with the breeze, tickling her nose. While she worked the guys talked in a steady hum. Her thoughts drifted to last night.

She could only imagine what it would feel like to sink into Brad's embrace, to feel the touch of his steady hand as he tenderly tilted her face to him and pressed his lips upon her own, warm and moist, the soft scratch of his evening whiskers—

"Look out!"

Brad's voice rattled her to attention. She turned in time to see one of the guys slipping on the plywood. His boots scraped against the wood; his body slid downward. With one hand she white knuckled the edge of the roof and with the other she clutched onto him in a viselike grip. Her hand was weak and shaky as she attempted to block the worker's fall. A man on the opposite side steadied him, and another near his ankles stopped him from plunging. He was able to get his footing on the ladder and make his way down. Everyone cheered. Men started congratulating Callie for her quick work.

She sought out Brad below, but he wasn't looking at her. Not that it mattered what he thought. He was a friend. Granted, a very good-looking friend, but still. The look on his face when he saw her new hair color had been priceless. To say that he was surprised would be an understatement.

There she went again. Thinking about a man

she hardly knew. She had been through the whole falling in love thing once, and she had told herself she wouldn't do it again. Maybe deep down she knew that was a promise she wouldn't keep—or hoped she wouldn't—but even though it had been two years since Jeremy, she wasn't sure she wanted to jump into a relationship again. Not that Brad was interested in her. A kiss was no big deal. Especially since the man was in pain. People do crazy things when they're in pain. Maybe once he healed, she'd have to trip him again.

She needed to keep her thoughts far from him or she could fall off the roof, too. Though something told her she was already falling.

"Are you all right?" Brad's voice was gruff, but she didn't miss the concern on his face.

"I'm fine."

He touched her arm. "You shouldn't have been on the roof. Leave it to those who are experienced."

She felt anger rise inside her. "I did okay." She put away her share of the tools.

"You did okay because you got lucky." His eyes blazed. "Don't do it again." He stomped off, leaving her and the crew gaping after him.

Her neck and face felt white-hot. If she were a poker, she'd brand him with a J for jerk.

"Don't worry about it. He was just worried

about you," one of the guys said. The others nodded.

Finished for the day, Callie went to her car, kicking dirt along the way. If Brad Sharp thought he could talk to her that way in front of the others and get away with it, he was wrong.

Dead wrong. The next time she saw Brad, she was going to give him a piece of her mind.

Once Callie reached her car, she clawed her way through her handbag for her cell phone.

"Hey, Aunt Bonnie."

"Hi, Callie. You off work now?"

"Yeah, that's why I'm calling. I'm headed home to let Chaos out, and then I'll be at the salon in time for my perm appointment."

"I hate it that you're having to work so hard." Aunt Bonnie's voice was thick with worry. "Would you like me to order a sandwich and have it waiting for you?"

"No, thanks. I'll grab one on the way."

When Callie stepped inside her place, the sight that greeted her told her she might want to turn around and go back to work. On second thought, if she had to choose between seeing Chaos or Brad, she'd choose her rebellious puppy, hands down.

"Chaos!" She had forgotten to put him in his crate before leaving for the day. Throwing her handbag on the kitchen table, she ran through the house. Toilet paper marked a white trail through the living room. Shredded remains of a doggie toy were scattered about. Chew marks ran clear through the toe of a favorite shoe. A sinking feeling settled in her stomach. "Chaos!" she called again, this time with more urgency, as she eyed the scattered debris. Just as she entered her bedroom, she spotted Chaos with a feather pillow in his mouth, his head twisting and jerking about playfully, long ears flapping with wild abandon, when a final rip in the pillow released an abundance of feathers into the room. "Chaos," she said once more, falling on her knees in utter despair.

He bounced up to her with delight. Feathers stuck to his fur, and he looked like a sparsely plucked chicken. Callie laughed in spite of it all—which only fueled his enthusiasm. His tail wagged furiously, and he jumped on her, tongue lapping endlessly, feathers scattering about.

She was quite upset over the state of her house, but the jumping and puppy joy completely won her over. She held Chaos close and wondered how in the world she would get everything picked up in time for her appointment. Reaching for the phone, she called Aunt Bonnie and explained what had happened, telling her she'd clean up the main problems and get there as soon as possible.

After hanging up, Callie stood and surveyed the

area with hands on her hips. "Well, we have a mess to clean." Chaos wasn't bothered in the least. In fact, he seemed quite pleased with this turn of events as she watched him trot down the hall as though to proudly display his afternoon shenanigans—just in case she had missed anything on her first walk-through.

She hated to admit it, but she knew that Chaos was spending too much time alone. The evidence was all around her.

What a day.

By the time Brad paid for the Chinese carryout and headed to his mom's, he had calmed down. Seeing Callie hanging on to that guy while she was only inches from the edge of the roof herself had caused fear to strike his gut. With his crutches in hand, all he could do was helplessly watch the drama unfold and pray for her safety. He sucked in a deep breath. He couldn't think about it anymore.

Clutching the bags and crutches, he leaned his elbow against the doorbell. His mom finally answered. "Brad, come on in."

The house wasn't much better but at least she was dressed and her hair was combed.

"I brought you some chicken broccoli," he said, lifting the bag. He wasn't going to ask her if she'd eaten. He knew better. And he also wasn't giving her a choice. If he had to spoon-feed her himself, he'd see that she ate something.

"You are worse than a mother, you know that?" she said with a grin. "You shouldn't have done that, honey, what with your ankle and all." She reached over and gave him a kiss on the cheek.

"Oh, I'm fine. It doesn't hurt so much today. I'm getting along pretty good. Should be able to get rid of these soon." He knocked his hand against a crutch. "Luckily, it was my left leg, so it doesn't affect my driving."

"Well, that part is good," she agreed while getting some glasses down from the cupboard for iced tea. "Thank you for dinner. What do I owe you?"

"A night out on the town with my best girl."

"Oh, you don't want to be seen with this old woman."

He walked over to her. "Sure, I do, Mom. I think you're beautiful." He pulled her to him and cringed at her thin body. He had to be careful how he approached things.

They sat down to dinner and he said grace for the meal.

"You still want to go see Grandma tonight?"

"That would be great."

She toyed with her food but ate some, so that made him feel a little better.

Once they got through the meal, she grabbed

her purse and Brad drove them over to the nursing home. Their heels clacked against the durable linoleum as they made their way to Gram's room. A man dragging a portable oxygen tank behind him shuffled up beside them and wanted to know if Brad's mom was married. The woman walking with him frowned and gave him a good whop on his head. "Ya hardly got any breath in ya, and you're still chasin' the women. Ya old goat." He tossed Annie a wink and Brad could see her trying not to smile.

"Well, look at you," Gram said when they entered her room. "Looks like you got in a fight and lost."

"Something like that," Brad said with a grin, taking long strides toward the bed. "It's dangerous out there."

"Don't I know it. That's why I stay in here." She chuckled. "Did you bring any goodies?"

Brad laughed, bent down and dropped a kiss on her forehead. She was all skin and bones. Wrinkles gathered in tiny bunches around her milky gray eyes and threaded lines through her cheeks. "What kind of goodies, Gram?"

"Chocolate. What woman doesn't want chocolate? Doesn't matter if we're nine or ninety, we want our chocolate." She scooted up in bed, as though preparing for a good debate. She poked a gnarled finger toward him. "And if a woman doesn't want chocolate? She needs help."

"Now, Gram, you know chocolate isn't good for you. All that sugar."

Grandma looked at his mom. "I'm telling you that doggone television has ruined kids today with all that nutrition mumbo jumbo." She turned back to him. "Maybe you haven't noticed, but I'm not exactly in the running for Miss America."

Brad laughed out loud. She was spry for ninety years old, he'd give her that. "Okay, I'll bring you chocolate the next time I come."

"Bring some for your mom, too. If she gets any skinnier, a strong western wind could blow her into Indiana." She patted the bed for him to come sit down beside her. "You married yet?"

He was halfway into his sit-down position when her question almost made him fall over. No beating around the bush, and she didn't have the daintiest of voices.

She chuckled. "Must have a live one on the line or I wouldn't have rattled you that way. It's time you get a good woman to help you settle down so you're not flitting all over the world."

A nursing-home attendant walked into the room and filled a pitcher with fresh water.

He groaned. "Oh, come on, Gram, not you, too."

"It's time you brought someone in here to meet me." There was that gnarled finger again, pointing at him.

"You might as well not fight it. I've known this woman long enough to know that when she points like that, it's all over. She has the will of a pit bull," the nursing attendant said.

He suddenly thought of a bazillion things at home he needed to tend to.

"So how are you feeling today, Mom?" Annie asked.

Gram started coughing and Brad mouthed a silent *thank you* to his mom.

When Gram's coughing settled down, she said, "Well, you can see I'm not ready to run a marathon, but I'm still kicking, so don't give away my crossword puzzles."

Brad laughed at his grandmother's spunk. She turned her attention to his mom.

"Annie, I'm serious about your weight. You need to eat. And your hair—"

"She's working on it, Gram. And I'm taking her to get her hair done soon," Brad said. Annie nodded.

"Ooh, I haven't had my hair done in years," Gram said wistfully.

For a second Brad thought about getting Callie

to come over and take care of Gram's hair. But could he trust Gram with Callie?

On second thought Gram's hair looked just fine the way it was.

Chapter Six

"Are you sure we have to walk, Chaos?" Callie could barely crawl, let alone walk. She had washed, colored, snipped and curled more hair today than she cared to think about. Was every kid in the town going to the prom tonight? Glancing at her hands, she groaned. Between building a house and working with hair, her hands were in need of some serious TLC.

She yawned and flopped into a chair. It was Saturday afternoon, and all she wanted was a hot bath—or at the very least a good book and a soft bed. Chaos jumped into the chair and thumped his front paws against Callie's chest, nearly taking her breath away. His tongue lapped her face furiously. He smelled of puppy food and baby shampoo.

"Okay, okay, I'll take you walking." Callie

pulled the happy pup away from her face. Chaos's stubby tail wiggled with wild enthusiasm, his big brown eyes joyful. Her heart warmed.

She hauled herself out of the chair, retrieved Chaos's leash and grabbed an energy bar on the way out the door. She had had no idea that owning an animal was such work. Although Callie loved Chaos fiercely, some days she wondered how she could manage it all. Single moms and dads had to be the world's greatest heroes of all time.

The smell of spring perfumed the air. As they made their way past the schoolyard, gas station and across the bridge, Callie began to feel life seep back into her tired body. The cool air did her good. The park near her home came alive with the laughter of children. Chaos jerked and pulled away from Callie, running straight for the kids, joining in the play. Amid giggles and cuddles, Chaos was in his element.

"Looks like they're having fun."

The deep voice caused a blip in Callie's pulse. She turned around to see Brad with a slight smile on his lips.

She couldn't ignore her anger, no matter how handsome he looked. "Hi, Brad." Her words were cool. "Where are your crutches?"

He shrugged. "Hammer needed to get out. I knew I couldn't manage him and the crutches."

Tail wagging, Hammer stood at Brad's feet, watching Chaos and the children.

"I see." An awkward pause hovered between them.

"Listen, about the roof thing yesterday, I shouldn't have talked to you that way."

"I quite agree."

"But I meant what I said."

"I may not be experienced, but I'm not afraid to try." Okay, maybe she was, but she wasn't going to tell him about her fear of heights. "And if it weren't for me, that man probably would have fallen."

"You're right. It's just that when I saw you—" He cleared his throat. "You're right."

He didn't go so far as to say he was sorry, but his apology was in there somewhere. She'd accept it. The fact that the look on his face melted her heart had nothing to do with it.

She turned to watch Chaos. "It seems puppies and children were made for each other. I wish I had that kind of energy."

"You're kidding, right?" Brad's dark eyes glistened in the afternoon sun. "You have more energy than a pot of brewed coffee."

She didn't know whether to be flattered or offended.

Hammer tugged at his leash. "Want to walk with us?" Brad asked. "Or should I say hobble with us?"

"I think you're doing pretty well, considering you hurt yourself just a couple of days ago," Callie said.

He swayed a moment and she steadied him with her hand. He turned to her.

"Thanks. You're good at catching guys when they fall."

Funny he should say that. She often thought she was good at catching, but not so good at being caught. She wished someone had caught her when she had fallen—or maybe she should say when she was dumped.

Jeremy had waited until the invitations were sent. Things were going fine until then—or so she had thought. But suddenly it was over. And it had taken her so long to move on. Past the embarrassment, the numbing grief, the shock, the loneliness. After the initial pain had subsided, she frequented their favorite coffee bar, as though something there would give her insight into what had happened, would heal the dull ache that never went away. But all it did was make her miss him even more.

She had finally worked past all that. Now the question was, what was she doing entertaining the possibility of another relationship? Especially with Dr. Jekyll and Mr. Hyde, who confused her as much as he captivated her.

Still, hadn't Heather told her she had to get on

with her life? And it wasn't as though she and Brad were dating or anything. Part of her hoped the friendship would grow, and another part of her said to run away as fast as she could. But so far her feet stayed planted—next to Brad.

"Let me get Chaos. I'll be right back." She ran over and scooped her puppy into her arms.

"Your dog is good with kids," Brad said when she came back.

Callie nuzzled into Chaos. "Yeah, he's great." She put Chaos down and they resumed walking.

"So, working on the house has probably been hard for you with your current salon schedule," he said when she came back.

"A little." Okay, maybe a lot, but she wasn't going to tell him. Not when things were just getting interesting.

"Sorry about that."

"It's my own fault. I guess you know I'm working there to pay my debt to society."

He grinned and rubbed his jaw. "I'd heard that somewhere."

"From your brother, perhaps?" She smiled up at him.

"I'll warn you. My brother is up to no good."

"I think he had a little help from my lawyer, Heather, who also happens to be my best friend."

Chaos stopped to sniff a flower. Callie tugged on the leash. She wanted no interruptions in this conversation whatsoever.

Brad shrugged. "Ryan likes to send single women my way—but don't get nervous. I won't bite you, I promise."

She wasn't so sure of that. "Let me guess. He's trying to marry you off?"

His eyebrow raised. "Don't tell me you get that, too?"

"From Heather, from my aunt, from my uncle..."

He shook his head. "Why is it everyone thinks we have to be married to be happy?"

"I don't know. Maybe because they're happy and they want that for us?" Saying "us" in that context made her cheeks warm, and she was pretty sure she saw little hearts with wings fluttering around his head. She ignored them.

"Or they're miserable and they think we should be, too."

The little hearts cracked in two and disappeared from sight. She took a deep breath. "Brad, I want to ask you about the other night—"

"Mr. Brad! Mr. Brad!"

They both turned to see Micah Sauders running toward them. Chaos yanked hard against his leash and broke free.

"Chaos, get back here," Callie yelled. But her

puppy scurried as fast as his little legs could carry him to his newfound friend.

Micah scooped him up and carried him back to Callie. Chaos licked her face the entire way while Micah giggled with delight.

A slight twinge of guilt played around Callie's heart. Chaos was alone all day and no doubt missed the companionship of people. Not that she could do anything to change that. She had to work. At least she took him out when she got home. That should help a little, she thought. Still, seeing the way he played with Micah, she wondered.

"Well, how are you, Micah?" Brad said.

"I'm having fun at the park with Mommy." Her eyes sparked with joyous energy.

Andrea Sauders walked up to them. "Hello, Brad, and—I'm sorry, I've forgotten your name."

"That's the lady with the nails in her mouth," Micah piped up.

Callie laughed. "Yeah, I guess that's me. Callie Easton." She extended her hand to Andrea. "Good to see you again."

They talked while Micah played with the dogs. Andrea explained that her husband, Mick, had lost his job and she was worried about qualifying for the house, but Brad assured her that as long as she had her job at the Burrow Diner and could make the payments, they were fine. Andrea looked relieved.

"They are such a wonderful family," Callie said once Andrea and Micah had left.

"Yes, they are. I'm thrilled they were able to get this house. Life has been challenging for them, but I've never, ever heard them complain."

Callie thought of all the times she complained about stupid things. Food, weight, work. She considered herself a positive person by nature, but she'd lost some of her sunny outlook after Jeremy walked out on her.

"It's a good thing we're doing," he said, turning to her when they reached the spot in the park where they would part ways.

She nodded.

"By the way, I like your hair like that." He reached up and touched a strand near her cheek, causing her nerves to wake up and stand at attention.

"Yeah?"

His eyes held hers. "Yeah." His fingers lingered at the side of her face. All thoughts of getting answers from him, or holding him accountable for his gruff ways, slipped from her mind.

"Thanks."

They said their goodbyes and turned in opposite directions to go home. She prayed her legs would hold her.

"Oh, one more thing."

She turned back around.

"I bought a croquet set for my mom. She lives alone, and I wanted to get her out of the house to do something fun. I'm setting it up tomorrow after church. Didn't know if you would want to come over and play."

Her heart leaped to her throat. The words could barely crawl over it. "That would be fun. I haven't played croquet in years."

"All the better. Gives me a chance to beat you."

She laughed.

"I'll swing by and pick you up around one-thirty. Will that work?"

"Sounds great."

He nodded and left. Somehow her rubbery legs got her home, though she might have floated home on the breeze. Just before euphoria could set in, she realized she hadn't given him her phone number or address. Would he have a list because she was a volunteer at the house? Would his brother have it? Maybe she'd better call Heather and tell her to let Judge Ryan know. No, that wouldn't work. She would sound desperate. Contacting him was definitely out of the question. She'd appear too eager.

Slow down, Callie. Take it easy. Protect yourself. Something told her she would never get to sleep tonight. No matter that only hours ago she had vowed never to talk to the man again. He had apologized—sort of—and she was obliged to forgive him. The Bible said so.

Besides, what could it hurt to play a harmless game of croquet together?

As people milled around in the foyer after church, Heather stalked over to Callie like a supermodel on a runway. "So what time is Lover Boy picking you up?"

"Would you stop that? Someone might hear you," Callie said with a frown. "He's not my boyfriend. He's just a friend." Though she had to admit she was glad she had used the salon's new volumizing shampoo this morning, and the root lifter was just the ticket to give her hair the extra oomph it needed.

Heather smirked. "Whatever." She examined her nails. "So what time?"

A glance at her own nails told her she'd need to apply another coat this afternoon. "Around one-thirty." Callie hiccupped.

Heather grinned. "Somebody's nervous."

"It's such a curse, the whole hiccup thing."

Heather chuckled. "I think it's charming."

"It's time to come clean, Heather. Did you and Judge Sharp plan the whole thing?"

Heather suddenly waved at some guy who appeared not to know her. "Gotta go! Lunch with my Sunday school class. Ta-ta!"

Callie almost laughed at her friend's transparent tactic. Looking around, she decided now was a good time to leave. She needed a moment to catch her breath before Brad came over. She'd managed to steer clear of her aunt and uncle all morning and was hoping to get out before they caught her, just to avoid any questions.

The pastor had talked about how God would never leave His children. Callie almost wondered if Aunt Bonnie had talked to him—his message went right along with their recent conversation. Callie knew it was true. It was just so hard to trust sometimes—to believe that God would never leave her. The truth was that when her mother died and her father left, she felt God had gone, too. Everything that had been right with her world was over. Aunt Bonnie had said Callie couldn't trust those feelings, and she knew that. Still, a sign from Heaven would be nice.

The foyer buzzed with the joyful chatter of friends who hadn't seen one another in a few days. Volunteers stood behind tables where members could sign up for various events. People waved goodbye to clustered groups still in the foyer, then exited the front doors, while children dashed back inside. It was a good time for her to slip away unnoticed.

"Callie."

Too late. She turned around. "Hi, Aunt Bonnie."

"Where have you been? I've been looking for you all morning. We wanted to see if you could come over for lunch."

"Oh, I—I— Well, I need to let Chaos out, and I had planned to do some reading." That excuse sounded lame even to her ears.

Aunt Bonnie's eyes narrowed to slits. "Oh? You're going to spend the afternoon reading?"

"I said I had planned to." Which was the truth. That was her plan before Brad had asked her to come over.

Not to be deterred, Aunt Bonnie cocked her head in such a way that Callie visualized her in a trench coat and dark glasses.

"What are you reading?"

"Bonnie, could you come over here for a minute?" one of her friends called.

Aunt Bonnie turned. "Yes, be right there."

"Thanks for the invitation. Maybe next week. I'll call you later." Callie reached over and gave her aunt a quick peck on the cheek. "Love ya."

"I'll deal with you later," Aunt Bonnie said suspiciously.

Callie laughed. "I've no doubt that you will."

After introductions Brad and Callie went outside to set up the croquet while his mom made lemonade. Once everything was in place, Brad and Callie slid into their seats at the patio table.

Looking over at her, he wondered if he'd let his conscience get the better of him. He could have apologized for his brusque behavior and forgotten the whole thing. He didn't need to invite her to his mom's house. Alarm shot through him. This was almost like a real date. Did she think this was a date? He tried to swallow but couldn't. He was doing the very thing he vowed he'd never do. Date one of Ryan's setups.

"Brad, did you use Google to stalk me?" Callie asked.

Brad looked at her, puzzled. "What do you mean?"

"How did you know where I lived?"

He smiled. "Ah. I have a whole file on you, Callie. Thanks to the justice system."

"Your mom seems like a nice lady," Callie said, obviously changing the subject, blushing in a very charming way.

Brad mentally shook himself. This was no big deal. Just two friends. Eating together. Playing croquet. What was the harm in that? "She is. Things have been tough on her since Dad's death, and then my sister's."

"You lost a sister?"

"Yeah. She died not long ago."

"I'm sorry."

"It's hit the family pretty hard. Been hardest on Mom, though, I think. I'm trying to get her to do things outside of the house." Why was he telling her all that?

"Here we go." Mom placed the tray of glasses in the middle of the table, picked up the pitcher and proceeded to pour. "It was nice of you to bring the croquet set, Brad. I haven't played in years." She placed the drinks in front of them.

"Thanks, Mom." He took a drink, the lemonade slightly tart but delicious. Made him think of summer. "It's unanimous, then. None of us has played for a while."

"Thank you, Mrs. Sharp." Callie took a sip.

"Oh, please, call me Annie."

Callie smiled. "Okay, then. Annie."

The phone rang inside. "Oh dear. I'll be right back." His mom ran into the house.

"So tell me about you." Callie's fingers toyed with the side of her glass.

Brad shifted in his seat. "What do you want to know?"

"Well, let's see, you build houses. You do a little remodeling on the side. What else do you do?"

"Isn't that enough?" He laughed.

"Yeah, it is." Callie laughed, too.

"Actually, I also travel in South America, working on homes for the underprivileged. That's what I love the most."

"Why is that?"

Her question surprised him. "I get to see beautiful country, learn other cultures and help people all at the same time."

"I don't mean to argue, but it seems to me we have plenty of people in need right here in our country."

He didn't know why, but her comment landed somewhere in the middle of his gut. "Well, that may be true, but I haven't seen many."

"No offense, but maybe you haven't looked hard enough. You don't have to look very far. Don't even have to look outside of Burrow."

"I don't exactly see the homeless on street corners in Burrow."

"No, that's true." Her words were calm, but passionate just the same. "Most are hanging around in shelters downtown. Since the decline in the glass industry, Burrow has seen its share of foreclosures. But I guess since you're in the house-building business, you already know that."

It was true—he hadn't been around all that much until recently. Still, she was taking on a martyr attitude, as though she and she alone cared about Burrow. He'd been born and raised here. She didn't have a corner on the town. Sure there were people in need here—every town had them—but there were also needs elsewhere.

"I'm not saying there aren't problems here in town. It's just that I believe there is more of a need to help in other countries." Why was he defending himself? He didn't owe her an explanation.

"Other countries where there is beautiful country and different cultures."

A twinkle danced in her eyes, but that didn't help him deal with his anger. "Look. I'm a firm believer that if you've got something to say, you need to say it."

Callie looked startled. "Oh, nothing. I'm sorry. I guess I just get a little passionate about my hometown. I think work in places like South America is desperately needed, but I also think we have plenty to do here at home. That's all." She sipped some more of her lemonade.

"I guess everyone has their calling."

She put her lemonade down. "Is that yours?"

He thought a minute. "I don't know if it's a calling, but it's where I want to work."

"That was your brother," his mom said, stepping through the patio door.

Brad tensed. Things just kept getting better.

"They're coming over."

Maybe he should go back to bed and start the day again.

Chapter Seven

"Hey, Brad, how's it going?" Ryan gave his brother a good-natured thump on the back. "This is a great idea. I haven't beaten you at croquet since we were kids. Have you gotten any better?"

Brad gave a half smile and walked over to straighten a couple of the wires that were now standing crooked in the grass. How many times had they played every sport imaginable in this very yard when they were growing up? His brother always won—he seemed to have the upper hand in just about everything.

Not that it was a contest. He just got tired of having to prove himself. Though sometimes he wondered if he did it for himself or for his brother.

"Oh, stop teasing your brother, Ryan," Brianna said. "Olivia, do you want to play?"

The teenager shook her head. "I'd show you all up."

"Just what makes you think I won't win?" Mom joined in.

Her boys exchanged a grin. "That's right, Mom. You'll probably whip us all," Brad said.

"By the way, Uncle Brad, I got a job."

"You did? Olive, that's great. Where are you going to work?"

"Peaches & Cream Ice Cream Parlor. I started last night."

Brad groaned inwardly. Another connection with Callie. Just what he needed.

"Yeah, and we get a discount," Brianna beamed.

"Not exactly big money, but at least she's got a job," Ryan said. "Olivia, if you're not going to play, now would be a good time to grab my laptop from the car and check out some of those college choices."

She pulled in a long breath and blew it out. "Okay, Dad." Looking a bit disappointed, she obediently walked toward the car.

"Why don't you give her a break once in a while?" Brad asked.

Ryan turned around, surprised. "What are you talking about? She has one more year before she's off to college. Most kids have their future mapped out by now."

"Most kids, or do you mean you?"

"What's that supposed to mean? I—"

Just then Callie walked out of the house. Ryan heard the screen door and looked her way. She took the rest of his words right from his mouth, which Brad figured was a good thing. He knew he was about to get the if-you-had-gone-to-college speech. But Brad didn't want to be Ryan. Maybe he should have gone to college, but he loved building homes. It came naturally to him. And he was good at it. So that was what he chose to do. He didn't know if Ryan was more upset with Brad's choice because he didn't educate himself or simply because he didn't follow Ryan's advice.

Brad turned to Callie and smiled. "Brianna, Ryan, Olive—this is Callie Easton."

Callie held up her hands. "No delinquent parking tickets, Judge Sharp, I promise."

Everyone laughed. Mom had no clue what was going on, but she laughed just the same, which Brad took as a good sign. He hadn't seen her truly laugh in some time.

"Olivia, nice to see you again. When Uncle George hired you, I didn't realize you were related to Brad," Callie said. Something in the way she said his name made Brad's skin tingle. He immediately stood.

"Ryan, let's go try out the croquet set," he said, needing to get away. Ryan agreed, and they crossed the lawn together.

"So, it's nice to see Callie here." Ryan hit the ball and smiled at his brother.

"Let it go, Ryan." Brad hit the ball a little too hard and it rolled too far to the right.

They continued the game without further discussion of Callie, for which Brad was grateful. After several rounds of croquet, Annie refilled the lemonade glasses and they settled on the patio.

"Callie, tell me about your work," Annie said.

"My aunt and uncle own the Peaches & Cream Salon, and I'm a hair stylist and manicurist there."

"Really?"

"She'd be a great one to fix your hair for you, Mom," Brad said. "She's who I had in mind when I was telling Gram I was going to take you to the salon."

Annie thought a moment. "*You're* Callie from the salon." Her eyes sparked with remembrance. "Nicole talked about you."

Callie was confused. "Nicole?"

"Nicole Gentry. She went to your salon to get her hair done. I remember her mentioning you."

"Oh, sure, I knew Nicole. How did you know her?"

Annie swallowed hard. "She was my daughter."

Callie's eyes grew wide. Her face turned the color of unpainted drywall.

"Oh, I'm so sorry. Nicole was a friend of mine."

The blood rushed from Brad's face. "Friend? How well did you know her?" He wasn't sure he really wanted to know, but he had to ask.

"We went out for coffee once in a while. Not real close friends, but friends." The sorrow in her voice, no doubt, spoke volumes to the others. Not so much to Brad. "I was so sorry to hear of her passing. I was away at a conference when it happened. I wasn't even sure how—"

"Anorexia," Brad snarled. Everyone looked at him. "She basically starved herself to death."

"Oh," Callie said, nodding.

"You're not surprised." His blood ran hot.

"No. I mean, I didn't know she was anorexic, but I thought she was very thin. And she never wanted to go to dinner. Even at the coffee shop, she always drank plain coffee, and very little at that."

He stood up. "Did you try to help her?" He couldn't help himself now—he was blind with fury.

She stiffened. "She told me she was getting a divorce. I figured she wasn't eating a lot because of stress. How could I have helped her?"

"Brad, sit down," Ryan said gently.

"Nicole needed help and no one saw it. And I'm sorry, Callie, but your salon only encouraged her in the sick pursuit of perfection. No one helped her," he repeated.

"Did you?" Callie asked calmly, quietly, the piercing, probing question hanging between them. The question that he'd run from ever since Nicole died. "Brad, just because a woman gets her hair or nails done doesn't means she's sick, or even that there's any problem. It just means she wants to feel beautiful. And there's nothing wrong with that."

He sat back down and said nothing.

Callie turned to his mom. "Annie, thank you so much. Unfortunately, it's time for me to go." Callie looked at the others. "So good to meet you. Olivia, I'll look forward to seeing you at the ice-cream parlor." With that, Callie turned and walked away.

"Wait, Callie. I'll take you home," Brad said.

"No, thank you. I can call a cab," Callie insisted.

He got up and followed her. "Look," he said quietly. "I didn't mean to sound so harsh, it's just that—"

"I understand." She cut him off in a way that said she didn't understand at all. "But I'd prefer to take a cab."

Fine. If that was the way she wanted it, so be it. He watched her walk down the driveway and away from the house, digging in her bag for her phone. He knew he should go after her, but pride and anger kept him rooted to the spot.

The sooner he got out of Burrow—and away from Callie Easton—the better.

Monday morning, the crew painted the walls all day. Brad hadn't said two personal words to Callie, which suited her just fine. He had sent her on errands and given her woodworking to stain, which managed to ruin her manicure. She was certain he was happy about that. He'd basically given her grunt work, which fueled her anger and made her work even harder. She would not give him the satisfaction of thinking she noticed.

She thought about their conversation about Nicole yesterday. He could hardly blame her for what had happened to his sister, and yet that's how he'd acted—as though it were her fault in some way. Clearly he was carrying around an awful lot of guilt and wanted to push it onto everyone else so he didn't have to face it himself. Well, she would not let him dump it on her.

Not that she hadn't cared about Nicole. The young woman had seemed troubled by her marriage, but she hadn't dwelled on it. In fact, had she not mentioned it to her, Callie probably would never have known Nicole was going through a tough time. Yes, she had thought Nicole was too thin, but a lot of women these days were thin. The culture dictated it. She didn't know Nicole well enough to realize that wasn't normal for her.

What was done was done. They couldn't fix things one way or the other. Nicole had made her choice, and there was nothing any of them could do.

At the end of the day, just as she was leaving, the Sauders family pulled up. Micah ran over to Brad and gave him a hug. Callie waved and headed for her car, but Micah ran to her.

"Miss Callie! Miss Callie!"

Callie turned around. "Hi, Micah."

"Come here. I have to talk to you and Mr. Brad." She grabbed Callie's hand and pulled her toward Brad.

"Wait, Micah, I can't—I need to go, really."

Micah kept pulling and trudging toward Brad. "Mr. Brad, come here."

Brad locked eyes with Callie and quickly looked away. "What's up, Micah?"

Hand in hand, Andrea and Mick joined them.

Micah sported her snaggletoothed grin, her eyes sparkling. "My class is having career day tomorrow." She could barely contain her excitement. "Mrs. Upton said we're supposed to bring someone in to talk about their jobs. I asked her if I could bring both of you, and she said yes!"

Micah clapped and hugged them both, not noticing that they were speechless.

"Um, Micah, they might not be able to, honey. They have to work, you know," Andrea said, "and we hardly gave them any notice."

Micah looked at her mom. "Oh, I know they will come. They're my friends." She turned to Brad and Callie. "You'll come, won't you?" Her expressive blue eyes said she had no doubt whatsoever that they would come.

How could Callie turn this sweet little girl down? "I would be happy to come, Micah," Callie said.

Micah looked at Brad.

"Me, too."

The eight-year-old jumped up and down a couple of times and squealed, "Group hug!"

Callie didn't dare look Brad's way when they narrowed their circle into a hug around Micah. She ignored the warmth of his arms around her shoulders, the woodsy smell of his cologne.

"Since it's in the afternoon and you work together, we thought you could bring Miss Callie with you," Andrea said to Brad.

If she didn't know better, Callie would say sweet little Andrea was in on the town conspiracy to get her and Brad together. Too bad she and Brad couldn't get along for more than two minutes at a time.

* * *

The following afternoon Callie climbed into Brad's truck, determined to keep her attitude in check. The upholstery squeaked beneath their weight. The door groaned shut. Though the truck was older and used to haul lumber and tools, Brad kept the inside clean. Too bad he wasn't as nice as his truck. Well, okay, he obviously had moments of goodness, like yesterday when he agreed to take time off from work to visit Micah's classroom.

Just when she wanted to be good and disgusted with him, he had to go and be nice. Brad messed with her mind, pure and simple. She would be glad when this project was over and she could be done with Brad Sharp for good.

"Thanks for running more errands today," Brad said.

Another nice moment? She wanted to tell him to knock it off.

"You're welcome." Her voice was normal, level, without commitment one way or the other.

He opened his mouth as though he were going to say something else, then decided against it. They rode the rest of the way to school in silence—she wasn't about to make this easy for him.

The room of second graders cheered the moment Brad and Callie stepped inside the classroom. A small red carpet had been rolled out, and a love seat dubbed "The King and Queen Chair" stood at the end of the aisle. Across the blackboard hung a banner with the notation "Heroes' Day." In the back corner of the room sat a long table with a large cake and punch on it.

Callie and Brad exchanged a surprised glance. They turned to find a giggling Micah Sauders beside them. She led them to the love seat.

Soon, school smells of chalk and glue sent Callie to another time, another place, where she endured the school day knowing her mom and dad wouldn't greet her when she got home. When other children laughed and ran about at recess, she hovered in schoolyard corners, alone with her thoughts and overwhelming grief. Her heart had ached beyond description in those dreadful days when tentacles of loneliness stretched around her heart and squeezed so tightly she could barely breathe. Even now the memory took her breath away.

She glanced at Brad and found him studying her. "You okay?"

She nodded and smiled, pretending all was right with her world. She would not allow her past to ruin Micah's special day.

Mrs. Upton, the teacher, introduced herself and explained "Heroes' Day." Each student was assigned a week to bring in a hero of his or her choosing. The only rule was that the hero couldn't be a relative. Micah had chosen two, which was an exception to the rule, but Mrs. Upton had bent the rules per Micah's pleading. Therefore, the class decided to crown Micah's heroes "King and Queen" for a day.

Brad and Callie leaned forward on the love seat as Micah excitedly slipped paper crowns onto their heads.

"Micah, would you please introduce the King and Queen for today?" Mrs. Upton took a seat at the back of the class so she could face Micah and her guests.

Dressed in a cute white shift with small red flowers and white leggings, Micah swayed back and forth as she told the class Brad and Callie's names.

"You may proceed with your talk, Micah," Mrs. Upton instructed kindly.

"Um, Mr. Brad is my king for today 'cause he's building a house for my family." She pushed a strand of hair away from her eyes. "His big fingers have rough bumps on them and Daddy says that's cause Mr. Brad works so hard for us. Daddy says we should thank God for him. So we pray for him every night." Micah fidgeted with her fingers for a moment. "Mr. Brad is always nice to me, and one time he bought me an ice-cream cone when the ice-cream truck went by. My mommy and daddy say Mr. Brad could make lots of money doing other things but he would rather build homes for families like us." Her tongue explored the corner of her mouth while her eyes searched the ceiling for more words. "He's our hero, and I'm glad Mr. Brad is here for my family." She gave a sharp nod of her head indicating she'd finished talking about Brad.

Callie could feel a lump form in her throat. Brad swallowed hard, then tossed a wink at Micah. What if he had been away when this project idea came up? Someone else would have done the work, but would he have made such an impression on this child?

"Miss Callie," Micah said, bringing Callie's attention back to her, "well, I don't know her so much." Micah turned to Callie. "But she has the prettiest smile I ever saw—next to my mommy. And she always smiles—especially when Mr. Brad is around," Micah added, to Callie's everlasting mortification. Muffled giggles rippled around the room. Micah turned a grin to Callie, once again melting Callie's heart. "She smells good and she has soft hands. She's building our house, too, though Daddy says she'd probably rather work on people's hair than their houses." Callie laughed at that. "She is a hero and a queen to me." Micah took a moment to smile at Callie and then turned back to the class.

"I can't wait to sleep in my new bedroom and

live in our new house. I will never forget how Mr. Brad and Miss Callie worked together to make it so special."

When Micah finished, her class clapped and cheered. She walked over and gave Callie and Brad hugs, then skipped back to her seat. Mrs. Upton proceeded to cut the cake and pass out drinks in honor of the guests. Micah's day was considered a huge success by Mrs. Upton's second-grade class at Burrow Elementary.

After the ceremony had ended, Brad and Callie walked back to the car. Once inside, Brad turned to Callie. "That's one special little girl," he said, putting the key in the ignition.

"Yes, she is."

"Listen, I know I've been a jerk, but—"

Callie held up her hand. "Let's not do this now, okay?" She didn't want to ruin the afternoon.

"Okay." He turned and started the engine. "I need to stop by the hardware store and pick up some more paint." His professional voice was back in place.

"All right," Callie said, matching his tone. When they arrived at the store, Callie said, "How about I look through the magazines while you get the paint, and I'll meet you at the register?"

Brad gave a curt nod and took off toward the paint aisle.

Callie flipped through pages of room remodels, lush garden sanctuaries and landscaping pictures before she noticed a magazine that really caught her attention. Picking it up, she took in the cover featuring a child's playhouse and flipped to the appropriate page to see more pictures of it. She imagined Micah in such a house. She was a grateful kid, with so very little in the way of material things—she would love it.

"Wouldn't Micah love that?" Brad was reading her thoughts, his breath warm against her shoulder.

When she turned to him, he seemed to realize how close they were and took two steps back. She could only hope he wouldn't sprain his ankle again.

"I was just thinking the same thing. A little girl's dream come true." After a moment she leaned toward the rack to put the magazine away.

"Wait," Brad said. "We could do it."

"Do what?"

"Build her a playhouse."

"Are you kidding?"

"Well, not until the house is finished, of course, but after that we could use Saturdays to work on the playhouse."

"Saturdays are sometimes busy for me," Callie said, wondering if this were some type of peace offering.

"I thought it would be best to do it together, since she honored us with that whole King and Queen business. It would mean more to her coming from both of us. I'm doing it for Micah."

He had clearly added that last comment so she would have no illusions about why they were getting together.

"I'm flexible with time, so we can get together whenever. We have our differences, but surely we're adult enough to work on this project?" His eyebrows raised as though he were challenging her.

"I'll do it," she said, "For Micah."

He stared deep into her eyes. "For Micah."

Chapter Eight

Callie had taken one step into her home when the phone rang. "Hello?" Chaos ran over and she scooped him onto her lap.

"Hi, sweetheart. Did you have a good day?"

Aunt Bonnie's voice made her feel instantly better. She explained to her aunt about her time at Micah's school, but left out any mention of Brad.

"What a precious little girl," Aunt Bonnie said. "I wanted to let you know that Brad's mom called the salon today."

"Oh?"

"She wants to schedule a shampoo and haircut for her mother-in-law at the nursing home, and wants you to call her." Her aunt rattled off the number.

"Okay, thanks. I'll give her a call."

Callie settled back onto the sofa and called

Brad's mom hesitating for a moment first, wondering how Brad would feel about it. She decided this actually wasn't any of his business.

"Hi, Annie. This is Callie Easton returning your call." Callie tried to ignore the twist in her stomach. The sooner she could get out of this whole mess with Brad, the better. If she didn't adore Micah Sauders, she never would have consented to helping with the playhouse.

"Oh, yes, Callie. Thank you so much for calling." Annie explained that her mother-in-law, Louise Sharp, needed a shampoo and haircut, and she wondered if Callie could come and take care of her. "She is bed-bound, so I'm not sure if you can do that. We would pay you extra for your trouble, of course."

"Yes, I can help her. I have an inflatable portable basin that would work just fine," Callie said. "I will need to contact the home and see what I need to do to get approved. Once I get that cleared, I'll call you to set up a time. Will that work?"

"Perfectly. Thank you so much," Annie said. "And Callie?"

"Yes."

"I just wanted to say about Brad… He means well. He wasn't blaming you for Nicole's death. He's just trying to make sense of it. You see, he was gone when Nicole died. When they were younger, he watched over her, protected her—especially once his dad died and his brother moved out." She paused. "Unfortunately, as my husband lay dying, he made Brad promise he'd take care of Nicole. I think that's one of the reasons Brad can't let it go. He feels he's failed—Nicole and his dad."

"I understand," Callie said.

"He really is a good young man. Just has a few issues to talk over with the Lord." She hesitated, then said, "I guess we all do."

Callie didn't know what to say to that. When it came to talking things over with the Lord, she'd been a little lax on a few issues herself.

"Well, I hope to see you soon," Annie said, clicking off.

Callie certainly hadn't seen that one coming. Maybe she and Brad had more in common than she realized.

With Hammer at his feet, Brad sagged onto the sofa and absently pet his dog. "I don't know what's the matter with me, Hammer. I just keep being a jerk to Callie, even though I don't want to." The dog twisted his head this way and that so Brad could scratch in just the right places.

"I know what happened to Nicole is not Callie's fault. Once Nicole set her mind to something, no one could stop her. Anyone close to her knew that." Hammer whined and nuzzled his nose deeper into Brad's hand.

"So why am I treating her this way?" Brad jumped up from the sofa and started to pace. Hammer snapped to attention and watched him. "I'll tell you why," Brad said. "She's dangerous." Hammer gave another uneasy whine. "Flashing those beautiful baby blues, that soft smile." He stopped and looked at his dog. "Trying to melt my resolve, that's what she's doing."

His scowl deepened as he crossed the living room floor. "I'll build that playhouse with her for Micah's sake, but I don't trust her. Oh, no. I've seen the likes of her before." More pacing. "I have plans," he bellowed, turning to Hammer, whose head was cocked to one side. "I *am* going back to South America, and no one is going to stop me."

He whipped around and stomped down the hall. "Least of all Callie Easton." A little voice in the back of his mind told him he was being a jerk again, but he ignored it.

While waiting at the stoplight the next afternoon, Callie called Heather. "You've been busy," she said when Heather answered.

"Well, hello to you, too." Heather chuckled. "Yeah, I finally finished that big trial. I was so ready. So what's going on with you and Brad?"

"Wow, no beating around the bush with you," Callie said.

"I haven't got the time."

"Well, there's nothing exciting to report." Callie pulled into the parking lot and climbed out of the car.

"How do you feel about that?"

"Oh, no, you don't. I'm not about to give you ammunition to use on me later, especially since I suspect you got me into this mess. You should have been a psychiatrist instead of a lawyer, you know that?"

"So I've been told," Heather replied.

"Well, just wanted to check in. I'll call you later." Callie knew Heather wanted her to analyze her feelings, but she just didn't want to do that—not yet.

Callie stepped through the door of the home and stopped at the information desk to ask for directions to Louise Sharp's room. She meandered through the hallways, smiling at the various residents along the way. Normally, nursing homes bothered her, but this one was new and like a hotel. Bright lighting, beautiful fixtures, fresh lemony smells, happy residents. Taking a deep breath, her heart lightened.

When she stepped into room 30, she spotted Annie Sharp sitting in a chair next to an elderly woman with mischief in her eyes.

"Hi, Annie," Callie said when she entered the room.

"Callie, good to see you." She smiled. "This is my mother-in-law, Louise Sharp."

Callie placed her bucket and inflatable basin on the bay-window ledge and walked over to Louise, extending her hand. "Nice to meet you."

Louise gave her the once-over. "Not too fat and not too skinny. That's good," she said, followed by a curt snap of her head.

"Mom, please."

"Well, it's true. Too many young girls these days are nothing but skin and bones. Just like our Nicole." Louise turned to Callie. "You look healthy. I like that." Louise winked and Callie decided that despite the woman's bluntness, she liked her.

"Thank you," Callie said with a grin. She turned to Annie, taking in the rumpled hair and clothes that said she didn't really care if she got out of bed or not. Callie's heart went out to the woman. This family had been through a lot, that was plain to see.

"Well, let's get this show on the road," Louise said.

Callie laughed. "All right." She grabbed her things and began inflating the portable basin with her air pump.

"My, my, the things they do today," Louise said in amazement, watching the basin spring to life.

"And to think I've gone with dirty hair for the past week without needing to."

Callie shot a look at Annie, who browsed through a magazine with disinterest.

"These old tired bones just don't work the way they used to." Louise gave a grunt as she sat up straighter.

"Well, this will fix you right up," Callie said cheerfully.

Once the basin was ready, she placed the opposite end of the tube that was attached to the basin into the bucket to deposit the rinse water. Callie then maneuvered Louise's bed to a flat position.

"You have any more pillows?" Callie asked.

The woman raised a crooked finger. "Over there in the closet."

Callie grabbed some pillows and propped them beneath the older woman's shoulders, so she would be comfortable.

"You sure know what you're doing," Louise said.

"I've been at it awhile," Callie said. She explained about her aunt and uncle owning the Peaches & Cream businesses, and her involvement in the salon and ice-cream parlor.

"That's where Ryan's girl is working, I think," Louise said.

Callie smiled and tested the water. "That's right. Olivia is a hard worker. We're thankful to have her."

"The Sharps are hard workers, every last one of them. Get it from their grandpa, not me. I'd rather take a nap." She chuckled.

Annie lifted tired eyes. "That's not true. You've been the hardest worker of all. Caring for your kids, working on the farm, holding things steady. How you juggled it all, I'll never know."

"You do what you gotta do. Oh, that feels nice," Louise said when Callie ran the warm water through her hair. "I forgot how good it was to have clean hair."

"I can't even find things in my purse, let alone balance my life," Callie said.

"I'd say you do pretty good if you're working at the salon, helping Brad and still washing an old lady's dirty hair."

"That's one way to look at it," Callie said.

"What do you think of our boy, by the way?"

"Now, Mom." Annie looked at Callie and rolled her eyes.

"Just wondering," Louise said.

"Brad is—is— He's a good delegator." That was the best she could do under the circumstances.

"Well, that tells us a lot right there," Louise said.

"I'm not sure I understand." Callie took extra time to massage Louise's scalp, certain the older woman didn't get such luxuries often.

"It was in your voice. You've had a falling out.

Not hard to imagine with Brad. He's a good boy. As thoughtful as they come. But don't get in his way or he'll run over you."

"Mom!" Annie scolded.

"Now, Annie, you know it's true. The boy has always been headstrong, right from the start."

Callie measured her words. She couldn't be too careful where Brad's grandma was concerned. She might be old, but she was sharp—so to speak. "Brad is a nice guy, and I appreciate that he's allowed me to work at the house."

"By the looks of you, I'm sure that wasn't a hard choice for him to make." The old woman's words were starting to slur as she relaxed. "You keep this up, young lady, and I'll put you in my will."

"You'll put who in your will?" Everyone turned toward the voice.

Callie locked eyes with Brad. And his eyes didn't look too friendly.

Brad wasn't sure if it was a mirage or truly Callie Easton standing in front of him, working on Gram's hair. Honestly, it seemed everywhere he turned, Callie was there. Sometimes physically. Sometimes only in his mind. But always there.

Why couldn't he shake her loose?

This was his brother's fault.

"Well, look who's here," Gram said with a chuckle. "Did you remember the chocolate this time?"

Brad said hello to his mom and walked over to Gram. He grabbed her hand. "Sorry, Gram, I forgot it."

His eyes flitted to Callie's, but she was focused on what she was doing.

Gram didn't reply, obviously enjoying her massage.

"What are you doing here?" he asked, trying to hide his frustration.

"Uh," Callie looked to Annie for help.

"I asked her to fix Gram's hair."

"You got a problem with that?" Gram asked. No doubt Callie was doing a good job and Gram wouldn't give her up easily.

"No, just wondered," he said pleasantly, not willing to take on three women by himself. Actually, fighting Gram alone was like taking on three women. "What are you getting fixed up for?"

"There's no law that says a girl can't look nice, is there?"

Once again he looked at Callie. This time she looked back, but when their eyes met, she turned away.

"No, I guess not."

"The hair stylist who had been coming into the

nursing home quit last week. Gram didn't want anyone else to wash her hair—until I told her about Callie," Brad's mom said.

Once Callie had the conditioner rinsed out of Gram's hair, she fluffed it with a towel, disposed of the water and put everything away.

"Would you like me to trim your hair for you?" Callie asked.

"Oh my, could you do that?" Gram asked. "I can't move much."

"Not a problem. I'll just shift your bed up and prop you forward enough for me to get to your hair." Callie pulled out her scissors and set to work on Gram's hair, careful not to allow the hair to get down her nightgown.

Brad didn't like the look in Gram's eyes one bit. And her smile told him that life as he knew it would never be the same.

Have mercy.

"How are you feeling, Mom?" Brad asked, trying to ignore Gram.

"Doing all right." Her appearance betrayed her words.

"You know, Annie, we got a new hair color in at the salon that I think would be perfect for you. I'll give you a free color treatment if you'll let me try it out on you," Callie said.

Annie hesitated.

Obviously, Callie could see that his mom needed a pick-me-up. He had to admit her kindness soothed his heart. "You can't beat an offer like that, Mom."

If you can't beat 'em, join 'em.

"I suppose not."

"Great," Callie said. "I'll call you when I get home, and we'll set up an appointment."

Brad was certain he saw his mom perk up a little. He turned to Callie. "You did a good job on the house trim this morning." He was careful to keep his voice controlled.

"Thanks."

That was it? Just "Thanks"? She obviously was still angry with him about what had happened on Sunday. Which bugged him a little. Okay, maybe they needed to clear the air. She hadn't wanted to talk about it yesterday, but maybe it was time, if they were ever going to…what?

"So, Brad, what are you going to do once this house is done? You going to leave us again?" Gram asked, subtle as always.

"I've got a remodeling job to do once the house is finished, before I make any major decisions," he said. "And you know I don't want to leave you, Gram. It's just that—"

"I know, I know. A man's gotta do what a man's gotta do." She turned her head down so Callie could snip the back near her neck. "Makes me wonder how your grandpa and I stayed in Burrow all these years without a thought of leaving."

"Everyone's different," Annie said.

"I guess. It's all those video games these kids play. You know what I'm talking about, Brad. You were glued to them when you were a kid."

He laughed. "Now, Gram, what does that have to do with me wanting to go back to my work?"

"Those games have you moving all the time. No one can sit still. It's spilled over into your adult life, you mark my words."

Callie grinned. Maybe she wasn't so mad at him after all.

He could almost feel the sweat breaking out on his forehead. It was enough that he had to finish this house project with her. Now he had to go and get himself tied up with her to make that playhouse for Micah. He was an idiot to suggest that. And now it appeared he would be running into her at the nursing home—if Gram had her way. Sometimes it seemed as though God were working against him.

Then again, it could just be Gram.

Chapter Nine

By the time Callie made it home that night, she was pooped. After Louise's hair, she'd had two more women from the home approach her and practically beg her to do the same for them. She caved. Others asked, but a staff member helped her get out of that—however, not before the administrator got her credentials and suggested she consider setting occasional appointments with the residents because it cheered them so much. Since she needed the money to do something for her aunt and uncle's anniversary, she quickly agreed, though she had no idea how she would find the time to squeeze in one more thing.

Callie walked to the bedroom to get Chaos. She hated keeping him in a crate, but the vet said it was the best place for him while she worked—that it would keep him out of trouble. After the mess he had made that one day, she knew it was true. Plus, she'd made sure she'd gotten a fine crate—large enough to move around in and to hold food and water bowls and a doggie blanket. When she stepped into her bedroom, Chaos jumped up, tail wagging a hundred miles an hour, paws doing a frantic shuffle.

Callie laughed, bracing herself for the slobbery licks that were sure to come fast and furious. Once again a pang of regret wound around her heart when she thought of how little time she spent at home. It didn't seem right to leave him alone so much. She blew out a sigh.

With Chaos outside, Callie slogged into the kitchen to search for something to eat. One glance inside the refrigerator told her it needed a thorough cleaning. Her nose wrinkled. A science project lurked within. She sighed. Disorganization followed her everywhere. Before she had time to sink into despair, the phone rang.

She thumped the fridge door closed and shuffled over to the phone.

"Hello?"

"I hope I didn't get you at a bad time."

Energy shot through her, causing all nerves to stand at attention. Brad's voice made her stomach flip. She wished it wouldn't do that.

"Oh, uh, no, no. What's up?" She tried to remember if he had ever called her at home before. Seemed as if that was something she would remember but sometimes it was hard to separate dreams from reality.

"I just wanted to thank you for helping Gram out tonight. You didn't have to do that." Did he think she had an ulterior motive? She tried to shake off the negative attitude. Something about Brad brought out her defensive side.

"I was glad to help. She seems like a nice woman." She settled in her favorite recliner-rocker.

"She's a sweet old woman. A little opinionated, but sweet." He chuckled.

She smiled, remembering his grandmother's curt but honest words. Callie suspected that deep down his grandmother had a heart of gold.

"So, why did you?"

Crickets and bullfrogs called softly just outside her open window. An evening breeze fluttered through the curtains. The night sounds always soothed her. And his voice…

"Callie?"

"Uh-huh."

"Why did you?"

"Why did I what?"

"Help her."

Her feet came to a halt, as did the rhythmic sway of the chair. His question surprised and perplexed her. "Your mom asked if I would go over and help her. There was no reason for me not to. So I did." The more she thought about his question, the more the simmering anger that had started in her stomach accelerated to a full boil.

"I just mean you're working plenty already."

Backpedaling. That's what he was doing now. *Oh, no, Brad Sharp, you are not getting out of this one so easily.*

"So are a lot of people." Her toe tapped steadily against the hardwood floor. The breeze now whipped her curtains with fury, the night sounds replaced by thunder. She ran to the door to get Chaos in from the rain.

Lightening pierced the sky, shattering the darkness with white jagged lines. Callie shoved the door closed and bolted the lock.

"It just seems odd. You don't even know my mom or my grandma—that's all I'm saying."

"That's not all you're saying. You're saying much more. So just get to it, Brad. Tell me exactly what you mean by that. We need to talk about a few things anyway."

"Just wondering why you're being so nice, that's all. I mean, you can't be doing it for me, since—"

"You're exactly right. I'm not doing it for you." She stomped over to the refrigerator, clunked ice into a cup and poured herself a glass of iced tea.

"That's what I mean. So why—"

"Are you this suspicious about everything? Do you think I want to get in good with your grandma to get to you?" she said sarcastically.

"People have been known to—"

"Are you kidding me? Don't flatter yourself. You're my supervisor on the job. Period."

"Listen, Callie, just calm down. I didn't mean it that way."

"Me, calm down? What is it with you and women?"

"What do you mean by that?" There was fire in his words.

"You run so hot and cold with me, Brad. One second you're kissing me, and the next you're accusing me of not helping your sister when she was sick. Are you trying to drive me away? Is that what you do when you like someone?"

"Oh, you've known me, what, two weeks, and suddenly you're the expert on my love life?"

The conversation was spiraling out of control, but she was too far gone to turn back now. "I'm just saying it's obvious you're not into commitments." She placed her iced tea on the stand beside her chair but was too agitated to sit.

"And you are? I don't see an engagement ring on your finger."

Okay, that one hurt. Did he know about Jeremy?

The whole town seemed to know he had walked out on her. But even Brad Sharp wouldn't—couldn't—be that cruel.

"Look, Brad, our work together is almost over. Can't we be civil until then?"

"What about the playhouse?"

She'd forgotten about Micah's playhouse. If it weren't for that precious little girl, there was nothing on this earth that could make her work alongside this man for one more day.

"Well?" he persisted.

She took a long, deep breath. "I'll do it for Micah." She hung up the phone.

Callie picked up her glass of iced tea but her hand was trembling, so she put it back down. Tears welled in her eyes and spilled down her cheeks. She cried tears of shame over her broken relationship with Jeremy. She cried over her confusing attraction to Brad, a man who could be as harsh as he could be nice. She cried over the lost parking tickets, and the fact that she had no money for a party for her aunt and uncle. Tears of regret and shame freely flowed as the rain pounded her rooftop in a torrent.

Callie knew of course that Jeremy had done the right thing. If he didn't love her, he shouldn't marry her. But pride was a ferocious beast, and she struggled to get rid of it, to cut loose from the pain she'd held so close for these past couple of years.

After her tears were spent, she was more determined than ever to keep her heart guarded. She'd been much too close to caring for Brad Sharp, and she'd been stupid. Never again would another man hurt her the way Jeremy had. No. Other. Man.

Brad punched his fist into the sofa pillow. "I don't get that woman at all!" he bellowed through the living room. Hammer glanced up and slunk out of the room. "Yeah, you'd better do that. You'd no doubt take her side. Traitor."

He grabbed a soda from the fridge in the kitchen, peeled the tab and flipped it into the trash. "All I did was ask her why she was being nice to Gram. A harmless question, and she blew it out of proportion." He stomped back into the living room. "Things always turn crazy when I talk to her. I just don't get it." He sagged into his chair and clicked on the remote.

"It's not like I thought she was after me. I didn't mean that at all. Though I can think of worse things." He blew out a frustrated sigh. "She just gets me all stirred up till I don't know what's heads or tails."

Flipping through the stations, he realized he

couldn't care less about watching TV, so he snapped the remote once more, turning off the television, and threw it on the sofa beside him.

As he slowly calmed down, he realized that in fact, Callie had been right on the money about a lot of things. He didn't want to get into a relationship that required a commitment. And he had indeed been giving her mixed signals.

He hated being wrong.

He'd get through the house and the playhouse, finish his remodeling job, then pack his bags and be on his way, as though his brother had never sent Callie Easton into his life.

Yeah, that was what he would do. Everything would be just fine. This would all be behind him, and they could both get on with their lives as they were meant to be.

Apart.

The painting was finished at the Saunderses' house, and the crew was supposed to be working on the punch list today—fixing any last-minute problems, making sure everything was working and ready for occupancy. They were almost done.

With the way things had been going, Callie needed a pick-me-up, so she'd taken extra care with her appearance today—it just made her feel more in control of her life. She was still reeling from Aunt Bonnie's friend pulling her into a corner at church yesterday to find out if she was planning to do anything for her aunt and uncle's thirty-fifth anniversary. When Callie had said yes, the woman suggested a caterer Callie couldn't possibly afford, and Callie had thanked her and then gotten out of there as fast as she could. She had no idea how she was going to swing the kind of party that Aunt Bonnie and Uncle George deserved.

Shaking her head, she walked into the house, where only a few people were finishing up. Brad turned around just as she stepped into the room.

"Brad? Should I call the paint store to see about returning those last two cans of paint?" one of the workers asked.

Brad stood there, staring at Callie. His expression might have been comical if she hadn't still been so angry with him, even several days later.

"Brad," the volunteer called again, with a knowing grin. "The paint?" He pointed toward the cans.

Glancing at him, Brad frowned and said, "Yeah, give them a call. Thanks." He turned back to Callie. "Hey."

"Hi." She looked around. "Where is everyone?"

Brad shoved a hand in his pocket and leaned on one leg. "Oh, I'm sorry. I should have told you not to come in today. We only need a few people to finish up the items on the punch list. You're free to go home."

"Can't beat that," someone said.

If she had known ahead of time, she might have scheduled some more appointments at the salon. Another reason to be annoyed.

Brad turned to the others. "Why don't you guys take a look at that door in the bedroom. I need to talk to Callie a minute." They nodded and headed for the bedroom, laughing among themselves.

The last thing Callie wanted was for the others to think there was anything between her and Brad. And she didn't want to have a private conversation with him. Things always got out of hand when they talked.

Brad led the way out of the house. "We'll be doing cleanup tomorrow, so you can come in for that. But your community time has already been served, so you don't *have* to come in."

"I told you, I finish what I start," Callie said, keeping a quick pace to her car. If at all possible, she wanted to cut this conversation short.

He placed his hand on her arm. She stopped walking and turned to face him. "Listen, Callie, can we start over?"

She just looked at him.

"I'm sorry about that thing with Gram. I know you didn't have an ulterior motive. I didn't mean to imply it. I don't know what I meant." He pulled off his hard hat and ran his hand through his hair. "We still have a playhouse to build together. Any chance we could call a truce to get through it?"

The sincerity in his eyes made her decide to give it a shot. "All right. We'll try. Again."

There was no denying she found Brad attractive. But there was obviously some bad chemistry between them, so she'd keep her mind on business when she was around him, ignoring the hard pounding against her ribs and the velvet brown of his eyes.

Her resolve was firm. She could do it. She just knew she could.

Brad headed back toward the house. The whole time he'd been talking to Callie about a truce, he'd been thinking about how beautiful she looked today.

He rubbed the back of his neck. He'd dated many women in his time, but none of them bugged him the way she did. Getting under his skin was her specialty. And she did it with such ease he didn't even know it until she was gone.

He'd gone soft—that's what he'd done. When she was around, he turned into someone else, someone who couldn't say what he was thinking.

He really didn't mean anything bad about her caring for Gram. It just came out all wrong. But that was the thing. He couldn't say anything right when she was around. She confused him. She'd walk into the room and his brain would scramble like knotted electrical wires.

They'd be civil and get through the playhouse project for Micah's sake and then part as friends, or acquaintances, or whatever it was that they were.

Yep. That was the plan. And he aimed to stick to it. Come what may.

Chapter Ten

"Hey, girl, I've missed you," Jessica said when Callie walked into the salon. "Seems we keep working at different times."

"I know." Callie began to set things up at her station.

Jessica joined her, a worry line etched between her brows. "You okay? You look tired."

"I'm fine. Just a lot on my mind. I'm trying to save some money for Aunt Bonnie and Uncle George's anniversary, and it's not working out so well."

Jessica walked back to her station. "Well, this might make you feel better—or not."

Callie looked up. "What is it?"

"I need someone to cover my appointments for a few days. My parents are headed to a bed-and-breakfast in Michigan, and they need me to house-sit."

"Wow, what's the occasion?"

"No occasion. Dad's just a romantic. Mom is feeling better, so he wanted to treat her." Jessica handed Callie a flyer about the bed-and-breakfast.

Callie gave a long, wistful sigh. "That is so cool. Your mom is lucky to have found a romantic guy like that. Wish they were all that way."

"Why do I get the feeling we're no longer talking about my mom and dad?"

Callie shrugged.

"Don't you worry. One of these days you and I will both find someone who will sweep us off our feet. You mark my words."

Callie gave her usual smile, feeling deep inside that it would never happen—at least not for her.

Jessica retrieved the flyer and went back to her station. "Anyway, Mom and Dad wanted me to house-sit, answer their business calls and take care of their two dogs. Since they live out of town, I'd have to get off work. I was wondering if you could cover my appointments, if you're not already booked. I wanted to throw it out to you before I told my clients. Since I knew you were trying to make money."

Callie grinned. "Oh, that would be great. That will help me a lot."

"What are you planning for your aunt and uncle anyway?" Jessica moved the products from her stand and swiped it with a rag.

"I don't know yet. I would love to send them to Hawaii. A big party would be nice, but I don't think I can afford that."

"Are those things they would want or things you *think* they would want?"

Callie paused. "You know, that's a good point. Maybe I'd better find out before I plan anything."

"They adore you, Callie. They'll be happy with whatever you give them."

Callie knew Jessica was right, but she still wanted to give them a great party, a gift, or trip. It was, really, the least she could do for them.

The next day, while Callie swept the living-room floor of the Sauderses' home, Brad took Mick through the house for a final inspection. It had to be frightening to move into a brand new home, knowing you had lost your job, but Mick looked excited. The Sauders were pretty amazing. Always smiling, always trusting.

Callie decided she needed to be more trusting. She'd gone to church with her aunt and uncle all her life. It wasn't that she didn't believe the stories of the Bible—she did. But life wasn't always that easy. Deep down she knew she harbored resentment toward God for not sparing her the pain Jeremy had caused. Guess she had expected God to change Jeremy's mind.

With determined strokes, she swished the broom hard across the floor. It wasn't fair to blame God. After all, she wouldn't want Jeremy just because God "made" him choose her. She wanted him to love her on his own. And he didn't.

The pain was easier now, of course. Her love for him had faded, but she clung to her resentment for some reason. It was as though she wanted to savor it, take it out and examine it, allow the sweet taste of self-righteousness to fill her mouth.

She swept up the dirt and sawdust, thinking about the Sauders and how much they would enjoy this home. Callie could almost hear Micah laughing and running into the room. What she hadn't expected was the vision of Chaos romping along behind her. Where had that come from?

"How you doing this morning?" Brad's voice startled her and she turned around.

That lazy grin again. She was so thankful he didn't know that that grin caused her heart to beat triple time and her face to burn like a heat lamp. Couldn't he do the decent thing and keep it hidden or something?

"Hi, Brad." She didn't know what else to say.

Mick Sauder stepped into view. "Hi, Mick," Callie said, thankful for the interruption.

"Good to see you, Callie." He turned to Brad. "Did you tell her our good news?"

"Not yet. You go ahead."

"I got a job," Mick said, grinning from ear to ear.

"That's wonderful, Mick," Callie said.

"Yeah, we're excited. I'll be working at the Burrow Tool & Die Factory, starting next week, making parts for them. I'll be on second shift, three to eleven, so if you guys need me for anything, keep that in mind, okay?"

"Will do," Brad said.

"Doesn't Andrea still work eight to five at the diner?"

"Just on Tuesdays and Thursdays," he said.

"What will you do about Micah?" Callie knew it was none of her business, but she couldn't help herself.

Mick dropped his gaze. "On those days, Micah will have to stay inside until Andrea gets home from work. She knows not to go outside or open the door for strangers," he said, as though reading Callie's mind. "Unfortunately, we can't afford a sitter. But Micah will be okay."

"I would love to have Micah with me," Callie blurted, before she had a chance to think it through.

Mick looked up. "But what about your work?"

"I could take her to the salon with me. Andrea goes right by there on her way home."

He looked at Brad, who was smiling. "The woman's got a point."

"I could even paint her nails, if you wouldn't mind," Callie said with a grin.

"She would love it. That's real nice of you, Callie. Let me talk to Andrea about it, but I'm sure she'll be crazy about the idea. We'll get back to you, okay?"

"Okay."

"Well, just wanted you to know about the job, so the powers that be won't be sorry they picked us for this house," Mick said to Brad.

"Never doubted it for a minute," Brad said.

Gratitude filled Mick's eyes. "See you guys later." Mick waved at the other workers who called out their goodbyes and stepped into the day's sunshine.

"That was real nice, what you did," Brad said.

The praise embarrassed her. "I just don't want Micah to be alone."

His eyes twinkled. "Callie Easton to the rescue."

His comment made her feel foolish until she looked into his eyes and saw admiration shining in them.

"If you need help, or if you get in a pinch and I'm available, I'll be glad to help." His gaze held hers.

Those brown eyes....

Someone called to Brad before Callie could comment. Which was a good thing, because she got the hiccups and quickly turned away.

She wondered just how she was going to add babysitting to her already full plate, but somehow she knew she could do it. And if she happened to need a little help, well, it was nice to know Brad was willing.

Following the cleanup at the Sauderses' home on Tuesday, Callie spent the next two days working at the salon. After work on Friday afternoon, she stopped by to check on the Sauderses' project.

The crew had leveled the soil, planted grass seed and shrubs. Not only was it the end of another workweek, but it was the end of another building project. Surprisingly, sadness tugged at Callie's heart. She took one last look at the home before getting into her car. Who could have known her lost parking tickets would turn into a blessing? She wouldn't trade the experience of building the Sauderses' home for anything. She'd had her struggles, but she had learned a lot.

"Hard to imagine it's over, isn't it?" Brad said, walking toward her.

She nodded and smiled.

"Every project is bittersweet. Bitter because you don't know if it's all going to come together, and sweet when it does and you get to see how happy you've made a family."

"Yeah, I see what you mean," Callie said.

"So, you're not sorry you had to serve time here?" She looked up at him and he winked.

She laughed. He really was trying to get along with her, and she needed to just enjoy his presence and stop trying to read into his comments or actions. "No, I'm not sorry."

"Good. I'm glad you helped. I mean, because you were a good worker and all—once you had your coffee and muffin anyway."

"Well, I'd better cut down on those muffins, or I'll have to start working out at the gym." As soon as she said that, she wished she hadn't. The last thing she wanted to discuss was anything that made him think of Nicole.

"I'd say the muffins haven't hurt you any."

"Thanks," she said quickly, hoping to move on.

"But if you're worried, I could help you out." That piqued her interest. "Oh, yeah?"

"Yeah." He scratched his whiskers and glanced at the sky. "Still plenty of daylight, and it just so happens I have two bikes at my house. How about we go for a ride?"

She was taken aback by his offer. A bike ride? The two of them? Weren't they still in truce mode? Although biking certainly didn't sound like a date. Sweating off the pounds was a far cry from a candlelit dinner. Sounded like a safe offer. "What kind of bikes do you have?"

"Road bikes. Good ones. I have mine and my sister's. I'm sure she would be pleased if you wanted to use hers." He studied her for a moment. "Of course, you're probably tired and hungry, and it's the last thing you want to do on a Friday night." He gave her a sideways glance. "You may even have plans already."

Was he digging for information? "No. No real plans." Too bad she had to admit that. "I think I might take you up on that bike ride. I've been out of the habit lately, and I can feel it."

"Are you hungry?" he asked.

"Not really. I'd rather eat later."

"Sounds good to me, too. We can grab something to eat after we're finished with the ride." His eyes searched her face again in a way that caused her tongue to stick to the roof of her mouth for a moment.

She hadn't exactly meant she would eat with him, though the idea appealed to her. She'd be careful, though. They'd been down this road before, with unpleasant results.

"I've got bottled water in the fridge at home. You can grab those while I pump up the tires."

Seeing the genuine pleasure in his eyes made Callie a little giddy. This would be fun. No entanglements, just enjoying the evening together as friends. This was actually a great idea.

Once they got to his house, Callie went to the kitchen to retrieve the bottled water while Brad worked in the garage on the bikes. A couple of food wrappers and spilt cola littered the counter. Tossing the papers into the trash, she grabbed the dishcloth and thoroughly cleaned the countertop. His home definitely needed a woman's touch.

She imagined herself standing over the stove, stirring his favorite ingredients together in a large skillet, a yummy scent permeating the kitchen. Brad would wrap his arms around her waist, turn her to him and… "Stop it," she told herself, throwing the cloth back into the sink and heading out to the garage.

"They look pretty good," Brad said, squeezing a tire. He saw her studying the bike.

It was hot pink. So typical of Nicole to get a hot-pink bike, Callie thought with a smile.

"Looks like something she would buy, doesn't it?" There was something very endearing in his voice when he talked about his sister. It was easy to see that Brad and Nicole had been very close.

"Yeah, it does."

"I still can't believe she's gone."

Callie was nervous about discussing Nicole. She held her tongue.

"Ride it around in the driveway and see what you think," he said.

"Okay." Callie slipped onto the bike and took a few trips around the driveway, feeling a tad self-conscious as Brad watched her. "Feels great," she said, coming to a stop near him.

"Good." He closed the door to the garage and climbed onto his bike. "This is a perfect area for riding," he said, leading the way. "Not many cars out here. We can pretty much ride side-by-side until a car comes along."

Callie nodded and pulled up beside him. The evening breeze fluttered through her hair, rejuvenating her senses. The air was sweet with the scent of honeysuckle.

"This is nice, Brad. Really nice," Callie said, taking a long, deep drink of the evening air. She turned to see him studying her. "What?"

"Nothing." Though he turned his focus toward the road, the look on his face told her he was having a good time, too.

"So, how is your mom doing?"

"Every day gets a little easier, I think. I have to keep after her, though," he said, his legs churning the pedals at a steady pace.

"How do you do that?" It impressed her that a man would take time for his mom that way.

"Oh, you know, just stop by and check on her, make sure she's eating, getting out into the fresh air. That type of thing."

"That's cool that you do that, Brad. Says a lot about you."

"Yeah?"

The grin on his face made her heart leap—again. "Yeah."

"So I'm not as bad as you thought I was before?"

"Well, let's just say, you're a better friend than boss," she teased.

"Hey, what do you mean by that?" He held his hand over his heart as though he were crushed.

"No coffee or muffin before work—any of this ringing a bell?"

"Come on, you can't blame me for that one. You were late, after all."

"That's true," she acquiesced with a laugh. "But those donuts you brought to the site. Where did you get those things?" She scrunched her nose.

"Were they that bad?"

"Only if you mind grinding mortar between your teeth first thing in the morning," she teased.

"As opposed to grinding mortar between your teeth later in the day?"

She laughed again.

"You have a nice laugh," he said.

The expression on his face made her uncomfortable. She waved her hand. "Oh, go on. I'll bet you say that to all the girls."

This time he laughed, and they trudged forward, to who knew where. The funny thing was Callie didn't care where. She didn't want to analyze anything. She just wanted to enjoy it.

As twilight crept over the countryside, she realized she was doing that very thing. Enjoying herself.

With Brad Sharp.

Chapter Eleven

"Hey, want to pull over?" Brad asked, pointing to a large tree by the edge of the road.

"What's the matter, can't keep up?" Callie teased.

"Hmm, do I hear a challenge in those words?"

She held up her hand. "No, no. I'm teasing—and very ready for a break."

They pedaled to the tree and settled beneath the canopy of the thick maple branches.

Callie leaned her head back against the trunk. "Oh, this is nice. I don't know when I've taken the time to do something so relaxing."

"I was just thinking the same thing." He looked at her. "This may surprise you, but some people actually say I tend to be a workaholic."

Her eyebrow arched. "Really? I hadn't noticed that about you."

"Are you making fun of me?"

She held her lips firmly together, eyes smiling.

"You're a hard worker, too, you know."

"I've been told that a few times."

Brad readjusted his position against the tree, inching away from her ever so slightly, and turned to her. "So, tell me about Callie Easton."

She smiled. "What do you want to know?"

His gaze searched the skies as he thought. "Well, for starters, you say your aunt and uncle raised you. Where are your parents—or should I not ask that?"

"No, it's all right." Callie told him about her mother's death, and how her dad had left. He heard the longing in her voice, the hole left by their absences, the faint shred of hope that her father would one day return.

"Wow, that's tough. I'm sorry, Callie."

They sat quietly for a moment. He turned to say something but noticed Callie's eyes were closed. A slight breeze stirred, rearranging the hair across her forehead.

She was beautiful, no denying that. Callie Easton possessed a natural beauty that no doubt few men could resist. He took in the long lashes, the shine of her hair, the shape of her face, the softness of her lips. What would it be like to feel them against his own? The last time he'd tried that, he'd been out of his mind on painkillers. For a moment he imagined it, longed for it.

Her eyes popped open. "Oh."

He blinked. Realizing he was too close to her face, he leaned back. "Sorry, I saw—there was something—I—"

Her mouth lifted at the corners, her eyes twinkling with amusement. She cocked her head to one side. "Yes?"

"You're gonna just sit there and let me dig myself into a hole, aren't you?"

She gave a shrug. "Something like that."

We're friends. We're friends. We're friends.

"So, why aren't you taken?" The look on her face made him wish he hadn't asked. "I'm sorry if I'm getting too personal."

"No, it's fine. I was in a relationship a couple of years ago." Her fingers worked through the grass around her, and she yanked a few pieces loose. "We were engaged and he called it off—after the invitations went out."

"Ouch."

"Exactly. It was a mess to clean up, and he left me to do it—alone." She threw the grass down and looked up at him. "End of story."

"So did he steal your heart forever? Make you lock it far, far away from anyone else?" *Better tread easily, Brad, ol' boy.*

She blinked and looked at him with surprise.
We're friends. We're friends.

She gave a slight grin but ignored his comment. "What about you? Anyone special?"

"Not really. I date occasionally but haven't met anyone I couldn't live without." The way she looked at him made him suddenly feel self-conscious. "I don't mean that to sound egotistical."

She laughed.

"Truth is, I've been so busy with life, I haven't had time to think about a relationship." *But now...*

Their gazes locked. For the life of him, he couldn't bring himself to turn away. The vulnerability in her eyes, the soft curve of her neck—she was...utterly irresistible. He leaned toward her, closer, closer....

We're friends.

His lips founds hers. He was lost in the softness of her skin, and his arms reached around her and pulled her closer. He tried to stop himself, but something about her made him hungry for more. His mouth pressed harder, searching, asking a million questions and not waiting for answers. The moment belonged to them. Callie Easton kissed him back in a way that told him maybe, just maybe, her heart was free from the man who had broken it two years ago. What that meant to him exactly, he didn't know. But he did know that this moment had changed him. Changed him in a way he couldn't describe. In a way that scared him. He wasn't sure what to do about it. But for now, it didn't matter.

For now, he was lost in her kiss.

He would deal with the questions…later.

When Callie pulled away from Brad, her hands were trembling. In an effort to still them, she folded them in her lap.

"I—" they said in unison. She smiled. "You first."

"No, ladies first."

Now she didn't know what to say. Wasn't even sure what she was going to say before. "Never mind."

"That was nice." That was all he said, but it was enough to send a warm flutter clear through her. That was not the response she had expected from him at all. Regret, shock, disappointment—those she'd expected. But "nice"? No.

So much for their friendship truce.

"Listen, Callie—"

Uh-oh, here it comes. The I'm-sorry-it-happened-and-it-won't-happen-again speech. "You know, it's getting late. We'd better be heading back," she said, standing. The last thing she wanted was for him to ruin the wonderful evening they had shared. Not now. Not tonight. Let her dream.

She went over to Nicole's bike, feeling Brad's eyes on her.

"You remind me of her, you know," Brad said.

"Who?"

"Nicole."

Okay, this was not how the scene had played out in her mind. In fact, the last thing she wanted to hear was that she reminded him of his sister.

"Sorry. It's just that she and I used to ride together and—oh, never mind."

"Is that why you want to leave?"

Confusion lined his face.

"To get away from the memories here?" To her way of thinking that was perfectly understandable, but the expression on his face said he didn't appreciate her remark.

"No," he said firmly. "I want to work in South America because I feel like I'm doing something worthwhile. Do you stick around Burrow because you hope that your dad will come back?"

The comment cut deeply. "No. I stick around because I don't believe we should abandon the people we love." Her eyes nailed him in place.

"Come on, Callie. You can't live your life for other people."

"I'm not living my life for other people. I

happen to love my aunt and uncle. I don't want to leave them. See, that's how it works. When you love someone, you stick around. You don't abandon them."

Her comments left no room for rebuttal. Seemed they couldn't get along for five minutes without arguing about something.

They rode back to his house in silence. It was just better that way.

Who did he think he was, telling her she was staying around in hopes that her dad would come back? Callie pulled on her nightclothes angrily.

It had nothing to do with her father. Sure, she hoped one day to see him again, but that wasn't what kept her here. It was the love of family. Other people applauded her loyalty to family and Burrow. Why couldn't Brad—or Jeremy—see that?

She didn't think ill of others when they left town. To each her own. But for her, she knew this was the right thing. She could never leave her aunt and uncle. She couldn't leave her beloved town of Burrow. It was everything familiar and everything she loved. Why did people have to change and leave? Why couldn't anyone appreciate the simple things in life?

Pulling down the thick comforter, she eased between the cool bedsheets. She supposed that's what went wrong between her and Jeremy. He had great ambition and didn't want to settle down in a "hick town," he had said. It had been a passing comment, a slight issue, but she hadn't realized it was weighing so heavily on his mind. She hadn't known he was planning to move right after they were married. When she found out, she thought that they could work it out—translation: that she could change his mind. She was wrong. Jeremy said it was a contract breaker—his words. She should have expected that from an attorney. Contracts and briefs were all he thought about. After he took a new position with a law firm in Boston, he'd met someone else and they married.

She tried to utter a prayer, but her heart wasn't in it. She was too upset. Besides, God seemed distant. Maybe He had moved, too.

She reached over and started the Itzhak Perlman CD. The one thing she had left of her mother, who had instilled in her a love for violin music. It was such a part of Callie now that she couldn't go to sleep without it.

She plumped the pillows behind her and tried to settle in. It was just as well that Jeremy had left. They were better off apart. She would find love again. But if she didn't, that was okay, too. Burrow was a wonderful place to live, and she couldn't be happier with her life.

If she had to live and die in Burrow as an old maid, so be it. She would not leave her family.

Period.

Brad jerked the cover down on his bed. "Running away from memories. That is ridiculous." Hammer whined as he watched Brad climb into bed and shove the pillows behind him.

"I want to do something with my life. Not stay in this town and rot. There's work to be done." Hammer barked at him. "See there, even you get that."

Brad wasn't running from anything. Callie hadn't shown him a psychology degree. What gave her the right to analyze him?

Truth seeped into the closed spaces of his heart, prying dark corners open. He did miss Nicole. There was no denying that. Tears filled his eyes. He had never cried over her.

He thought of Ryan and how his need to control drove him nuts. Had Nicole felt that way about Brad? He was trying to help her, but did he control her too much? Maybe he drove her to that jerk who broke her heart and changed the course of her life.

He was glad no one could see him. Only Hammer knew the truth. The pain scarred him. Guilt plagued him. He failed her. He failed his dad. How could he stay in Burrow? No one would dare say to his face that he had let her down, but he knew what they thought. No one would expect him to stay in town and face that day after day.

So maybe there was some truth to what Callie said, but it was none of her business. Yes, he cared about her more than he wanted to admit—he couldn't deny that—but a different path awaited him. Different dreams, different ambitions. Different lives.

After the house dedication on Monday, Callie headed for the nursing home to style Gram Sharp's hair. She thought about how the Sauders family had cried when Brad had presented them with their key to the house. The prayer over the family was highly emotional for all who knew them and knew what a blessing the house would be to them. Callie counted it a true privilege to have worked on the project.

"There's my girl," Gram said when Callie walked into the room.

Callie grinned. "Have you been behaving yourself?"

"Now why would I want to do that?" The old woman let out an ornery laugh. The more that Callie had gotten to know Brad's Gram, the more she grew to love her. In the brief time she'd known her, though, Callie could see Gram was growing more frail. She wondered if the older woman's health was failing but didn't feel it was her place to ask. Brad had been busy working on another house, and things had been strained between them since their bike ride, so she couldn't ask him. They were finally starting on Micah's playhouse tonight—maybe she'd bring it up, depending on how things went.

"So, what would you like me to do with your hair today?" Callie asked Gram.

The old woman shook her head and said with labored breath, "Not today, dear. I hope you don't mind that I didn't call to cancel, but I had hoped to at least visit with you. I could use the company."

The seriousness on Gram's face worried Callie. She pulled a chair up to the hospital bed and rested her hand on Gram's arm. "You all right?"

"Oh, you know, this old bag of bones just doesn't want to do what it used to."

"I'm sorry." She stroked Gram's thin, spotted skin.

Gram shrugged. "Just part of growing old. But I've got a better place to go, anyway."

Callie didn't know what to say.

"You know about it, don't you, sweetie?" Gram's milky gray eyes searched Callie's.

"Yes, Gram, I know," Callie said softly.

Gram brightened. "I knew it. Somehow when you walked in that door the first time, I knew it would be you."

"What do you mean?"

"For Brad. I knew you would be the one to straighten him out."

Uneasiness filled her. The last thing she wanted to talk about was Brad, especially with his grandmother. And what did she mean by "straighten him out"?

"Would you like me to open the blinds for you?" Callie asked, already walking toward the window. "A little bright light might cheer you up."

Gram chuckled softly. "Trying to change the subject, eh?" She straightened the sheet over her chest. "Probably just as well. I called Brad and asked him to come visit me. He should be here any minute."

Callie whipped around. "You called him to come over during my appointment with you?" Her eyes narrowed. "Gram, if I didn't know better, I would say you were trying to play matchmaker."

"Just wanted to have my favorite people around."

Her comment warmed Callie, though she still planned to make a hasty exit before Brad got there.

Too late. Callie's breath stuck in her throat when she saw Brad and Annie in the doorway.

"Hello, Callie." The haircut and color Callie had given Annie Sharp did her a world of good. She was an attractive woman, but life had strained her joy, making her look older than her years, Callie suspected.

"Hi, Annie. How are you?"

The woman brightened. "I'm doing better every day, thanks to you and Brad."

Callie cast a glance his way, then looked back at Annie.

"How so?"

"You've helped me care again. About life. I'd pretty much given up."

Callie walked over and grabbed her hand. "I understand."

"The doctor put me on some medicine that seems to help." She leaned in to Callie. "And I'm seeing a counselor to help me with Nicole's death."

Callie gave Annie a hug. "I'm so glad you're getting some help." When she let go, she saw Brad watching them.

"So, how was the dedication this morning?" Gram asked.

"It went well, don't you think, Callie?" Brad studied her in a way that caused her stomach to flutter.

"Yes, it was wonderful."

Brad went on to explain the events of the morning and how the house couldn't have gone to a more well-deserving family.

"Yet you're still ready to go," Gram said with obvious disappointment.

He frowned at Callie, then looked back at Gram. "Why do you say that?"

Her bony shoulders lifted in a weary shrug. "You always seem to be chompin' at the bit to get out of here, that's all."

"Now, Gram, you behave yourself." He tried to joke it off, but Callie could sense his tension, just the same. "I haven't been given my next assignment yet. I've got plenty of time."

Gram seemed to relax. "That's nice to know." She reached over and patted his hand. "I like having you around."

Callie didn't dare look at him. He would think she had put Gram up to it, for sure.

"I like it, too," Annie said. "But I know you've got to do what you've got to do."

"Thanks, Mom."

"And what is that, Brad?" Gram asked.

Callie could sense that Brad felt as if they were all ganging up on him. The conversation suddenly seemed uncomfortable.

Before he could speak, Callie said, "We have

to go where our dreams take us—or leave us." Callie smiled at Gram. "Where did your dreams take you?" She kept her eyes firmly fixed on Gram, though every square inch of her was aware of Brad's gaze upon her.

"To Brad's grandpa. Oh, I didn't care where we lived. We lived here because we grew up here. In those days we didn't flit off to other places on every whim." She turned to Brad. "Not implying that that's what you're doing, Brad. I know you're helping people, and that's good. The important thing is to make sure you're doing it for the right reasons."

Every nerve in Callie's body tensed. It was as though Gram had eavesdropped on their conversation.

"But my dream was to work alongside the man I loved and to build a family," Gram continued. "And that's what we did."

"You've had a good life, haven't you, Mom?" Annie asked.

"It's been a great life." She lifted that gnarled finger. "And it ain't over yet."

Later, when Callie walked out to her car, she thought about Gram's words. That's the kind of life Aunt Bonnie and Uncle George had. They didn't go to faraway places, but they had each other. They were living their dream—being together.

Maybe one day she could have that.

Chapter Twelve

"So how does it feel to be finished with your community service?" Heather asked as they jogged together after work.

"Great." The ache in Callie's heart told her otherwise, but she'd get over it.

Heather gave her a sideways glance, and Callie searched for another topic of conversation. Her friend knew her all too well, and she wasn't up to a conversation about Brad today.

"Any plans for tonight?" Callie asked, ignoring the knowing look on Heather's face.

Heather gave a nonchalant shrug. "Got a date with a new guy in town."

Callie shook her head. "You have all the luck."

"Yeah, right. Do you know how tired I get of the dating scene? Sometimes I just want to say forget it and not even try anymore."

"Can we take a break? I need some water," Callie said, slowing her pace.

"Sure. We can sit on that patch of grass over there," Heather said, pointing.

"Great." Callie pulled her water bottle from her backpack and held the cold drink against her face and neck.

"It is warm today, but it's almost summer so I guess we should expect it." Heather took a long swig of her water.

"So who's this guy?" Callie said with a smile, refreshed from her drink and enjoying the rest.

Heather frowned. "How come we can talk about my dating life but not yours?"

"Oh, that's easy—yours is much more exciting."

"Well, not much to tell. He's single. He heard I was single, and I think he needs a friend because he's new in town." She shrugged again. "He seems nice enough."

"Wish I could do that," Callie said.

"Do what?"

"Have noncommittal relationships."

"Isn't that what you and Brad are doing?" Heather asked, putting the cap back on her bottled water.

Callie let out a long sigh. "Supposedly."

"Uh-oh, what's that mean?" Heather stretched her legs out in front of her.

"Just that we try to stay friends, but then something always happens."

"Such as?"

Callie looked at her.

"Listen, Cal, we're good friends. Good friends are supposed to dig for information. You have to share. That comes with the deal. So spill it."

Callie chuckled. "It's just that we say we're going to be friends, then we have a disagreement over something and then he kisses me and confuses everything—"

"Wait, whoa, stop right there." Heather turned to her with eager eyes. "You're saying that Brad Sharp kissed you, and you didn't tell me about it? I can't believe this."

"I'm sorry, Heather. I just haven't been able to talk about it. Everything is so confusing."

Heather studied her. "You really care about him, don't you?"

Callie hated to answer that, but it was true. "Yeah," she said, defeated by the admission.

Heather took another drink. "Well, I'm not seeing the problem here."

Callie turned to her, tears blurring her vision. "It would never work. He wants to traipse around the world, building homes for people, never settling down. I'm not about that, and you know it. I'm a homebody. I would never leave my family. Besides, there's plenty to do right here in Burrow."

"That's true enough. I guess I was wrong. You're not in love, after all."

Heather's words irritated Callie. "Why do you say that?"

"Well, the way I hear it, when you love someone, you're willing to do most anything."

"Well, the way I hear it, if someone loves you, they wouldn't ask you to do something you were dead set against."

"True love is patient, kind, not self-seeking," Heather said with an irritating smile.

"To use your term, 'whatever.'" Callie got up. "I need to get back and check on Chaos."

"Okay, okay, I'm sorry." Heather stood. "Still, it's something to think about."

Callie said nothing. She was tired of trying to explain herself. It was her business where she chose to live her life. And she could manage it on her own, thank you very much. Well, okay, so she wasn't doing such a great job just now. But still.

"So, how's Chaos?" Heather asked as they started to jog again.

Callie knew that was Heather's way of smoothing things over. "He's doing all right, I guess."

"That doesn't sound very convincing."

"I just feel guilty leaving him so much. Now

that the Sauderses' home is finished, I should be home a little more, but still he's alone most of the day. Not much of a life for a puppy."

Heather seemed to weigh her words. "You could always give him away."

Callie looked at her. "Is that what everyone does? When things get hard, just walk away?"

Heather stopped jogging and put her hands on her hips. "Are we still talking about your dog?"

Callie ran her hand through her hair. Her mood was in the gutter, and she didn't know why she was so upset.

Heather sighed. "Listen, Cal, sometimes the best thing to do is to offer your loved one a better chance."

"Is that what you think he did, offered me a better chance?" Tears pooled in her eyes, but she didn't care. "My dad just left me, Heather, when I needed him most. Mom was gone and it hurt something fierce, but having Dad beside me helped. Then he walked away and never looked back. How could he do that?" She brushed the tears away with annoyance. She didn't want to be weak. Everything was bothering her all of a sudden.

Heather reached out to her, putting her hand on her shoulder. "I don't know. But we don't always know why people do the things they do. You want to give Chaos a better life, and that might mean a different home for him. Maybe your dad thought he could never give you the life you deserved, and he knew his brother-in-law and sister could."

"So why didn't he ever contact me?" Tears spilled down her face now.

"Oh, Callie." Heather pulled her into a hug, allowing her to cry till she was spent. "Are you okay?"

Callie nodded, cleaning her face with tattered tissue from her pocket. "All these years of waiting."

"I know," Heather said. "People show love in different ways. But whatever his reason, good or bad, you've got to let it go. It's eating you up."

Callie thought of that statement all the way home. *People show love in different ways.* How did she show love?

"So, how's it going?" Ryan grabbed a wooden chair. The legs scraped against the hardwood floor as he sat at the table with Brad at The Beanie Cup coffee shop.

A steady stream of customers kept the line going while a few retirees sat in cozy corners with the morning paper spread out before them. The whir and grinding of coffee beans hummed under the morning pleasantries between customers.

"Pretty good." Brad was suspicious. Ryan had

called and asked Brad to meet him. Brad wondered what could be so important that it couldn't wait until later. Usually when Ryan set up a get-together, he was prying into Brad's life.

"Yeah?" Ryan pulled the lid off his coffee and blew on it. "They sure make these hot."

Brad took a drink from his latte. "What's up?"

Ryan looked puzzled. "Can't a guy meet with his brother without an agenda?"

"Sure he can. But I've never known you to do that."

For a moment Brad thought he saw a flutter of pain in Ryan's eyes. He wished he hadn't said that.

Ryan sighed. "Look, Brad, I know sometimes you think I'm overstepping my bounds with you, but it's always because I'm trying to help in some way, okay?"

"Yeah, I know." Brad didn't really want to have this discussion. He had a job to get to. The painters would be at the new job site soon. Then he wanted to drop in on the Sauders later, when they were home. Callie had been watching Micah, but Mick had told him that Andrea's hours were getting changed at the diner and she would soon be able to be home with her daughter. He was glad. Callie already had a lot on her plate.

Callie. Always Callie. Did she have to consume his every waking thought?

"Brad, did you hear what I said?" Ryan stared at him.

"Huh? Oh, sorry." He shook his head. "Just thinking about some things."

Ryan leaned back in his chair and studied him. That always made Brad uncomfortable. Ryan was up to something. He could feel it.

"I hear you're doing a great job on the Make a Home projects. You're finishing up your third house now, right?"

"Yeah. I've enjoyed it."

"You're a gifted carpenter, Brad. Great supervisor, too, from what I hear."

Brad almost fell off his chair. His brother was a no-nonsense kind of guy, not big on praise. "Thanks."

Ryan leaned into the table. "What would you think of doing this on a full-time basis?"

Brad nearly choked on his latte. "What—what do you mean?"

"Just that some of the businessmen in town think it's a great service to the community. They want to donate more, make it a major community project. Help our own—that kind of thing."

Brad stared so hard he practically put a hole through his brother. Had Callie talked to him, too? Or maybe Gram?

Ryan studied him. "They'd like you to head up

the projects here in town." He smiled as though he'd just found the solution to world hunger.

"You know I want to build homes in third-world countries, Ryan. I really enjoy doing that work."

Ryan shrugged. "This is the same thing, only on your own turf."

Brad rubbed his jaw unconvinced.

"If it's just a matter of helping others, you could do that here, right? Or is it that you want to travel?"

Ryan was trying to pin him down, make him come to terms with his motive. That's exactly what drove him crazy. He didn't owe an explanation to anyone.

"All I ask is that you think about it. This whole concept is in the beginning stages. You don't have to make a decision overnight. But within the next month or two, they'll need an answer," Ryan said.

"I can tell you now," Brad began.

Ryan held up his hand. "Think about it. More important, pray about it."

Brad could hardly argue that. He would pray about it, but his gut told him he was already on the right track. He'd just allow some time to lapse so Ryan wouldn't badger him about it. Then he'd be home free.

Soon he could get on with his life.

* * *

Strolling up the sidewalk to the Sauderses' new home, Callie could see why Brad loved helping people this way. It gave life meaning. She was glad she had decided to rearrange her work schedule so she could watch Micah at her home. It was only for a few hours a week. She could do that.

"Chaos, no." Callie tugged the leash so Chaos would stay on the sidewalk and not track dirt into their home.

The Sauderses' yard was still leveled dirt, but Callie spotted a few sprouts of grass poking through here and there. Hopefully, they'd have a lush lawn by next year. Still, the house looked fresh, new and polished. Perfect for their little family.

Callie rang the doorbell and watched at the window to make sure Micah looked before opening, which she did. When she saw Callie, her face lit up.

"Hi, Miss Callie." Micah's face still wore that out-of-school-for-the-summer glow. Her eagerness made it all worthwhile—the extra hours she had to make up at work, the missed sleep, all of it.

"Hi, Micah. I have a surprise for you." Callie pulled on the leash and Chaos padded into view.

"Chaos!" Micah squealed and scooped the dog into her arms while Callie edged past them through the front door. It was easy to see who was important around here.

It appeared Andrea and Mick had been quite busy. Everything seemed pretty much in place, with only a couple of unpacked boxes here and there. The smell of fresh paint still scented the air.

Going through their normal routine, Callie fixed mac and cheese for Micah while Micah romped with Chaos in the living room. Andrea showed up earlier than expected, which worked out well, since Callie had to get to the salon for an appointment.

"Are we all set for the weekend? With Micah going to her grandmother's for the week?" Callie whispered.

"Yes, we're all set." Andrea smiled. "Her grandparents can hardly wait to have her. Though they're only three hours away, it's hard for them to come visit. They will have a great time. And she will be so surprised when she gets back and finds the playhouse." Andrea's eyes sparkled. "You and Brad will make a little girl very happy."

"She makes us very happy," Callie said quietly.

"Would you like us to watch your dog tonight while you go to work?" Andrea asked.

"We can watch her dog?" Micah started jumping up and down, which caused Chaos to do the same.

"Micah, settle down," her mother said. "It's up to Miss Callie. I merely offered."

"Could Chaos spend the night, Mommy, please?"

"It's up to Miss Callie. I told you."

"You're okay with that?" Callie asked.

Andrea brightened. "Sure we are. We love Chaos. He's like one of the family."

"He is trained, but you'll have to watch him. When he's ready to go outside, he'll let you know, but he's not real patient." Callie laughed.

"No problem. We'll watch."

"Well, if you're all right with it—"

Before she could say any more, Micah threw up her hands and shouted, "Yay!" She and Chaos ran around the room together, clearly happy at this unexpected turn of events.

Andrea turned to her. "Looks to me as though it's all settled."

"I guess so. I won't be able to pick him up until tomorrow after I get finished at the salon. You're sure that's okay?"

"Yes, that's fine. Mick will be here till I get home, so we have it covered."

"See you tomorrow, then." Callie shouted goodbye to Chaos, but he barely glanced her way. He was off and running down the hall with Micah.

When Callie got home from the salon, she called Brad. "Hey, Brad. I just wanted to call and let you know that Andrea said everything was set for this weekend. Micah will be gone next week, so we can get that playhouse finished. Mick will help us when he is home, too." Holding the cordless phone next to her ear, she paced the floor.

"That's great. I had hoped we could get started on it soon. I need to get this lumber out of my garage so I can fit my truck inside. Thanks for letting me know."

"You're welcome. I'll talk to you later."

Before she could hang up, he asked, "How have you been?"

The question caught her off guard. "I'm fine. Uh, and you?"

"Keeping busy with house construction. Sure could have used your help on this one."

"Oh, yeah, right. Like I was a big help. I didn't know the first thing about building when your brother put me there."

"You learned a few things, though. That's what's important."

She wanted to say, *Yeah, I learned a few things, like how I'd better hide my heart the next time around.* But of course, she didn't. "I guess."

"You could always lose some more parking tickets."

Thoughts of the ticket lurking in her handbag made her choke. She started to cough as she retrieved her handbag.

"Didn't mean to get you all choked up. You don't have to lose your tickets. It was just an idea to get you back on my job site."

She let out a nervous laugh while she rummaged through her bag in search of the ticket.

"What's that noise?"

"What noise?" she asked, picking her way through the various pockets.

"I don't know. It sounds like a squirrel digging his way through a pack of acorns."

She gasped and stopped searching. Irresponsible, once again. Hopefully Judge Sharp wouldn't find out.

"Oh, listen, Brad, I'd better go." She had to find that parking ticket or Heather would have her head. "I'll see you on Friday at the Sauderses' house, okay?" Opening her appointment book, she said, "My last haircut is at four-thirty, so I could be at their house around six o'clock. How's that?"

"Sounds great. I'll look forward to seeing you then."

She clicked off and stared at the phone, repeating Brad's words, "'I'll look forward to seeing you then.' He could have said, 'I'll see you then.' But he didn't. He said, 'I'll *look forward* to seeing you then.'"

Placing the phone back in its cradle, she realized she was grinning to herself. Apparently she was never going to learn.

Chapter Thirteen

When Callie's last highlight appointment walked out of the Peaches & Cream Salon, she scrubbed the black basin with a vengeance to remove filmy hair product. "Boy, am I tired," she said, straightening.

"You've been working too hard, Callie. You're going to have to slow down." Jessica had her hands on her hips.

Callie grinned. "Okay, Aunt Bonnie." She wasn't about to tell Jessica the weariness came from a lack of sleep. It was one thing to say she wouldn't think of Brad anymore, but it was quite another to comply.

Jessica frowned. "Make fun of me if you will, but when you come down with something, don't blame me."

"You worry too much." Callie put away the cleaning supplies, grabbed a broom and walked over to her workstation. With short strokes, she pulled the cut hair into a pile for easy pick up. Callie and Brad had such different ways of looking at things, yet he drew her in ways she couldn't explain. In a different way than Jeremy had.

She was attracted to him, but it was more than that. Much more.

She found Jessica staring at her and scrambled to say something. "Now that the Sauderses' home is finished, my schedule is more manageable."

"Yeah? So how come I never catch you at home anymore?"

"I didn't know you called. Why didn't you leave a message?"

She shrugged. "Nothing important. Just called to chat."

Callie squatted and swept the hair into the dustpan. "Hey, you never did bring in pictures of that bed-and-breakfast your parents liked so much."

"Actually, I did. I showed them to Bonnie, and she was very interested. Even mentioned she had an anniversary coming up and maybe they'd check it out."

Callie tossed the hair shavings into the trash and turned to her. "Really?"

Jessica nodded with a smile.

Callie thought a moment. "Guess I'd better look into it."

"It's worth a shot," Jessica said.

With a glance at the clock, Callie said, "Well, I'll be back in a couple of hours for my next appointment. Aunt Bonnie should be here any minute. I'm headed over to the nursing home."

Jessica shook her head. "Like I said, you're too busy."

"See you later, Mom," Callie called over her shoulder.

White-haired folks sat at round tables, playing cards and talking among themselves. A man at one table boasted of his win while several of the women shook their heads and grinned. A couple of people waved at Callie as she made her way past. One old geezer whistled at her. She laughed. They might be old, but they still had plenty of life left in them.

As she neared the end of the room, a man stood to his feet and belted out a blustery chorus of "Take Me Out to the Ballgame." Callie turned and listened. When he finished, everyone gave a hearty round of applause. Oh, to live life with that kind of abandon. Just to enjoy yourself and not worry about what people thought.

Not that she worried about what people

thought—well, except for Brad. It irritated her that his opinion mattered. But it did.

The next couple of hours passed quickly with a steady stream of white hair falling to the floor around her. Callie popped in to say hello to Gram, but she was sleeping, so she left a note and headed back to the salon. She would soon have a pretty good wad of money saved for her aunt and uncle's anniversary. Keeping up this work pace was getting old, but she would definitely miss the nursing home members when she stopped working there. And though it was understood she was there only temporarily, she decided she wouldn't stop before she found a replacement stylist. She owed them that much.

After she finished at the salon, Callie stopped in at the Peaches & Cream Ice Cream Parlor to see if Olivia was working. A blast of cold air hit Callie the moment she stepped onto the black-and-white checkered tile in the parlor. The red wood and chrome tables and chairs reminded her more of a soda shop than an ice cream parlor, but Aunt Bonnie had insisted on the furnishings.

Spotting the pretty girl behind the counter, Callie said, "Hey, Olivia, how's it going?"

Wiping the countertop, Olivia looked up with a smile. "Hi, Callie."

"So, you enjoying your new job?"

"I love it," she said enthusiastically. "And I get free ice cream." She leaned in. "I can say that since no one else is in here."

Callie laughed. "It does have its perks."

"So what are you up to?" Olivia asked.

"Just leaving work. Gonna go home and make dinner."

"How's it going with Uncle Brad?"

Callie's breath caught in her throat. The surprise must have shown on her face.

"Oh, I'm sorry. Should I not have said that? It's just that you look so cute together, and I've never seen Uncle Brad so in love before."

It was all Callie could do to keep her jaw shut.

"Uh-oh. I said something I shouldn't have." Olivia looked uncomfortable. "You didn't know?"

Though she knew that no one else was in the room, Callie looked around once more for good measure. The last thing she wanted was gossip about her and Brad to spread through the town. "Know what?"

"That Uncle Brad was in love with you?"

Callie dug deep into her lungs for a bit of air and tried to appear normal so Olivia couldn't see the emotional storm she was causing. "We're just good friends, honey," she managed.

Olivia's eyebrows raised. "Okay. Whatever you say."

Callie willed herself to be calm, but her body wasn't cooperating. "Listen, I've got to go. I just wanted to say hello." She hoped her manner appeared nonchalant. Forcing a smile, she began to back away.

"You're not mad at me, are you, Callie?"

"No, no. Of course not. I need to stop by the store before I go home." Another forced smile and a wave. "Talk to you later." Her voice was chipper, denying the chaos inside her. She formed slow and deliberate steps toward the door, ignoring her sweaty palms and trying to hide the hiccups that bubbled to the surface.

Olivia was just a kid. She probably fell in love at least twice a week. How could she possibly know Brad's heart? Callie's fingers trembled on the steering wheel and she hiccupped. Why couldn't she be like normal people and just deal with stress without sounding like a drain with plumbing problems?

Callie's emotions were in a shambles by the time she reached the grocery store. If she didn't need dog food, she would have skipped the stop all together.

She'd calmed down a little by the time she had pushed her cart into the produce section. She figured she might as well pick up a few things while she was there. She was rummaging through the grape bags for a good clump when a voice called behind her.

"You just never know who you're going to run into at the store."

Tiny shivers ran up her spine. Familiar shivers. When she turned around, her nose practically thumped into Brad's chest.

If she "ran into" him one more time, she was going to accuse him of following her. Not that she minded.

He barely stepped back. His nearness made her self-conscious. She couldn't back up because the produce was right behind her. He had definitely invaded her space.

She dared not look into his eyes. "Brad, what are you doing here?" She spoke the words squarely into his shirt.

"Aren't I allowed?"

The words rumbled in his chest, with the beat of his heart providing a steady background rhythm. She eased to the side and looked up at him. He grinned. The gleam in his eyes, the confidence, the determination—it all unnerved her in a big way.

She let out a nervous laugh.

"I just never expected to see you shopping at a grocery store. You know, since you never cook." As she teased him, the muscles in the back of her neck loosened. She reached up to brush a strand of hair behind her ear.

He grabbed her hand in midair and looked at her nails. "Coral, right?"

She tried to swallow. but her mouth got all dry and gritty.

"The nail polish. Seems I remember you telling me that once." Another lazy grin.

Somehow she managed not to gulp out loud. She made a mental note that coral worked for her.

"I'm going fishing. Thought I'd take some soda along with me, maybe a snack to tide me over till dinner."

"Where are you going fishing?"

"The riverbank down from my house." He hesitated. "Want to join me?" Amusement clearly shined in his eyes. "Unless of course you don't think you can handle it. Some girls get squeamish."

She was not a "girl." And yes, she could handle it just fine, thank you very much. Her chin lifted. "Sure, why not. I've never been fishing, but I'm game," she said bravely.

"The way I see it," he said, practically rocking on his heels, "there's no time like the present to get started." He winked at her.

Was this the same guy she couldn't get along with?

"Don't I need a license?"

He rubbed his jaw. "Actually, you should have one. Why don't we see if you like it first? If the gaming guys come around, I'll pay the fine."

Did she just agree to go fishing with Brad? If she could keep her mind off anything more than friendship, they'd get along just fine. Olivia's words came back to her. That was a big "if."

"Good. I'll swing by my house and grab an extra pole. Nothing fancy. Just your basic stick with a line. Why don't you meet me at my house, and we'll walk."

By the time they were ready, Callie wondered what had gotten into her. Not only had she never fished, but also she hated worms. She had hoped Brad would use a more sophisticated type of bait but her hopes sank like a broken bobber when he pulled out the box of worms.

Callie tried not to think about it as she followed him toward their place on the riverbank beneath a big oak tree. As the sun slipped slowly from the sky, splinters of light sprayed through tree branches and settled softly upon the water's surface. Birds fluttered and chirped, but otherwise the only thing that could be heard was the gentle rustle of the river.

"The first thing we have to do is bait the hook," Brad said with a grin.

Callie tried not to gulp out loud. *I can do this. I can do this.*

"Want me to help you?"

She could almost hear the drumroll in her head. This man traveled internationally. Probably ate chicken's feet and octopus, and wrestled crocodiles and plate-sized spiders. She could not—and would not—squirm at the sight of a worm.

"No, I think I can handle it."

"You're sure?" He looked at her as though he had his doubts, which fueled her determination all the more. She could almost hear a band playing a triumphant tune in the background.

"I'm sure." Taking a discreet but very deep breath, she opened the box of worms. There were hundreds of them, crawling all over one another, leaving slime everywhere. She'd never liked worms. As a kid, Johnny Barker used to chase her with them. The little twirp. He probably owned the fishing shop where Brad got them.

The one thing she never understood was which end was the head of the worm. Not that it mattered. She swallowed. Hard. One more time for good measure.

"You sure?" he asked again.

If she didn't know better, she'd swear she saw his mouth quiver, as though he was trying to hide laughter. She straightened.

"Yes, I'm sure." Pushing the disgust deep inside her, she cheerfully smiled at Brad while plunging her hand into the box. She acted as though she were merely reaching for a soda from the ice chest, all the while choking back her urge to scream loud enough to strip the bark from the trees. She pulled out the fattest, slimiest, wiggliest worm she had ever seen in her life. Her stomach lurched, but her pasted smile stayed, well, pasted.

That irritating grin still lurked at the sides of his mouth.

She looked at the worm, and then at Brad. Suddenly she saw a slight resemblance.

She grabbed the fishing rod and with trembling fingers lifted the worm—and hiccupped.

She dropped the worm back into the box, for which she was thankful. No doubt the worm was, too.

Brad laughed. "I was waiting on that."

Callie wanted to be mad, but the way he said it made her laugh, too.

"Here, let me help you."

He baited her hook and soon they were both playing the waiting game. For the life of her, Callie could not understand what people found so great about fishing. Going through all that gross, slimy stuff just to wait for a scaly fish to wiggle about on the end of your hook? Hadn't these people ever heard of fish sandwiches at fast-food restaurants?

"So, do you clean your fish and cook it?" she asked.

"I clean it but I don't cook it. Mom does that for me. I'm not a cook, remember? The only time I go into the kitchen is for snacks."

"Oh, that's right." Callie thought of Uncle George and figured he'd get along just fine with Brad.

"I hear you're quite the baker." He reeled in his line and recast it upon the water.

"Where did you hear that?"

"Gram."

Callie chuckled. "I brought her a piece of cake once or twice. Figured she could use some meat on her bones."

He looked at her. "I think so, too." Brad turned his attention back to his bobber. "I'm worried about her. She doesn't seem herself lately."

"I've noticed that."

"Thanks for making time for her. You don't have to do that."

"She's my friend," Callie said, meaning it.

"Thanks, just the same."

Callie's pole started dancing. "Wow, I've got something!"

"Reel it in nice and easy," he said. "Not too fast, not too slow."

"Oh, sure, that tells me a lot," she squealed.

Brad got up and moved behind her, placing his

strong arms around her; his calloused hands covered hers. "Like this," he said, reeling slowly on the bobber. "Feels like a good-sized catch," he said, yanking on the line, little by little.

Callie thought maybe she could grow to like this after all. His hands were warm and protective. The musty smell of his cologne overpowered the fishy smell of the river. It seemed he didn't stick with the same cologne for long. Unpredictable. She liked that in a man.

Once he pulled the fish out of the water, she couldn't believe the size of it. It was enough to feed a family of eight—okay, five. Well, it was certainly enough to feed both of them.

"Oh, you caught a walleye. Great job," he said. "I wasn't sure if it was too late in the season for them."

He held the fish up to her. "This is how you take it off. Put your hand on it like this so you won't get stuck by its fins."

Brad was so close, holding her hand as he helped her maneuver the fish free from the line. Fishing wasn't so bad after all.

They stayed another hour and caught three walleyes—well, she caught one and he caught two.

"Hey, I've got an idea. How about I clean the fish and you fry it up for us? Wouldn't take long." His eyes studied hers. "You should get to enjoy it, too."

With their past history, she wasn't about to accept—they'd just end up fighting again. She looked up at him and he was watching her with hopeful eyes…eyes the color of coffee beans.

"My house or yours?"

Chapter Fourteen

By the time Callie got back to Brad's place with the groceries, Brad had finished cleaning the fish. And he had on different clothes.

"Hey, no fair. You got cleaned up," Callie said, pleased that he wanted to look nice for her and even more pleased that she'd touched up while in the car.

"I was in worse shape than you. Fish stench was clinging to my clothes."

So much for looking nice for her.

He took a bag of groceries from her, pulled the items out and placed them on the counter.

"Would you turn the oven on for me?" she asked.

"We're not frying the fish?"

She shook her head. "Trust me on this. It's just as good baked, without all the calories and bad fat."

"I like bad fat."

"It doesn't like you."

He frowned. "Okay, but if I don't like it, we'll have to go fishing again." He bent down to turn the oven on. "It's only fair. By the way, I can't guarantee the oven works. I don't think I've ever used it."

"You're kidding."

"That is pretty bad, isn't it?"

"Yep." She grinned and began chopping up green onions. "Make yourself useful and help me out here."

"You want me to cook—in the kitchen?"

"It will be good for you. I won't make you put on an apron, I promise." She handed him the mushrooms. "I need about a cup of these, sliced."

When the onions and mushrooms were ready, Callie sprayed the baking dish with oil, spread the onions and mushrooms over the bottom of the pan and placed the fish on top. She seasoned with salt, pepper and marjoram, then sprinkled with lemon juice, cheese and crackers, drizzling melted butter on the whole thing.

"Wow, you're pretty good at this stuff."

"I told you, I like to cook. Now, step aside, mister." Callie put the pan into the oven, then brushed her hands together. "We'll be eating in about ten minutes."

"Great." Brad grabbed some paper plates and put them on the table.

"Using your best china, huh?"

His hand stopped in midair, paper plate still between his fingers. "Should I use real plates?"

She laughed. "I guess this means there's no hope for a centerpiece?"

To Callie's surprise he said, "Oh, now that one I can handle." He walked over to a cabinet and pulled out two brass holders for tapered candles. Heat warmed her face. She certainly hadn't meant for them to eat by candlelight. She watched as he lit them, looking rather proud of himself. "How's that?"

"Perfect," she said, trying not to laugh at the paper plates and fancy candles on the same table.

When the ice was in the glasses and the table set, Callie pulled the fish out of the oven. She scooped up the servings, and just as she added a sprig of parsley to each plate, she heard the soft music playing in the other room. This was beginning to feel more and more like a real date. But of course, it was just two friends having a nice dinner. Together. By candlelight. With music.

Over dinner, they each tried carefully to avoid the subjects that seemed to always bring about arguments. Callie had noticed a photograph of Brad and Nicole, and she started to say something but stopped herself. She didn't want to risk bringing her up.

Brad was clearly protective of his sister's memory and greatly affected by her death. The depth of his compassion for others moved her. Most guys were into themselves and their own interests, but Brad was willing to spend his life doing good for others. Funny how she could admire that and resent it all at the same time.

"So, where are you?" he asked when they settled on his sofa after dinner.

She blinked. "My mind is a blank screen."

A smile played on the corners of his mouth. "Wouldn't touch that one with a ten-foot pole."

She laughed. "Smart man." She was suddenly very aware of his closeness. "You know, I really should go. We have a big day tomorrow, what with the playhouse work tomorrow night."

Disappointment shadowed his face. "Do you have to?"

His question made her heart flip, but she ignored it—well, she tried to, anyway. "Yeah, I really do." It was far too dangerous sitting here with him like this. She didn't want to mess things up—again.

She walked over to the door and turned to him. "I just wanted to say thanks for a fun evening."

He put his hands on her arms, without so much as the slightest blink. "My pleasure. I mean that."

She gulped—discreetly, she hoped. "See you later."

Using every ounce of willpower she had, she turned and walked into the night.

* * *

"Hey, Cal."

"Hi, Heather. Did you get your Starbucks coffee yet?"

"It's in my hand as we speak," she said with a laugh. "How about you? Did you get your peach scone?"

"Not only was it in my hand—it is now history," Callie said, walking toward the salon.

"You're so lucky to have the bakery right by the salon so you can get there in the mornings."

"I don't know if lucky is the right word. I have to work doubly hard on the treadmill."

"Yeah, whatever. Listen, Cal, I had an idea."

"Uh-oh, why does that make me nervous?"

"No clue. You're the one who gets into trouble— you know, like not paying your parking tickets."

Callie cringed. "So what's up?"

"Well, you know how you've been talking about your dad a lot lately?"

Callie's stomach clenched. "Yeah?"

"I got to thinking, why don't you look him up? It's fairly easy these days with the Internet at your disposal. I could help you if you want me to."

Something didn't feel right, though she couldn't put her finger on what. "No, I don't think so, Heather."

"Why?"

"I don't know. If he doesn't seek me, there must be a reason."

"Okay. Just thought I'd throw it out there and see what you thought. If you ever change your mind, let me know. I'd be glad to help."

"Thanks."

"I'm at the office now. Talk to you later, girlfriend."

Callie stepped into the salon. The truth was Callie had thought about finding her dad before, but the last thing she needed was more rejection. Besides, she had all the men she could handle in her life right now. She was struggling as it was.

"How about coming over for dinner tonight," Bonnie asked after saying goodbye to a customer.

"I can't tonight." Callie hated to tell her aunt about working on the playhouse with Brad, but she knew her aunt would get it out of her.

"Oh?" Bonnie's eyebrows raised, hope lighting her eyes.

Callie refused to encourage her. "I've got some work to do." Maybe Aunt Bonnie would leave it at that, but Callie doubted it.

"What kind of work?"

"Just work."

A smile that she didn't even try to hide lit her face. Callie wondered if Aunt Bonnie's imagination was off and running. She could have the wedding invitations ordered by nightfall if Callie didn't tell her the truth.

"All right, all right. It's nothing to get excited about. I'm going to the Sauderses' house to help Brad build a playhouse for Micah while she's at her grandparents'."

"Oh." Such a little word, but she packed it with a wallop of meaning. Callie had half a notion to scramble the nail polishes around in Aunt Bonnie's manicure station. That would teach her.

"Well, for goodness' sake, keep me posted." Her chuckle resembled the happy tinkling of wedding bells. She probably did that on purpose.

By the time Callie got to the Sauderses' house, Brad had already built the outer frame in the backyard. "I can't believe you did that already," Callie said.

"I had some extra time today to work on it." Brad handed a rake to Callie.

"Thanks for letting me be a part of it, Brad," Callie said, brushing the hair from her eyes as she surveyed the yard.

"Of course you should be a part of it. Micah is crazy about you."

Brad used a shovel to level out lumpy places before Callie raked over it. Once they finished, Brad checked the frame's foundation with a carpenter's level on top of the rim joists. They then moved the frame away and spread a sheet of black plastic over the site to prevent vegetation from growing. Once that was done, they moved the frame back into place.

Brad stretched his back, looking at their work.

"You want to call it a day?" Callie asked. She was tired from working all day—she figured he must be, too.

He blew out a sigh. "Yeah, I think I'd better. I've got an early day tomorrow."

"You're as bad as me, you know. We're both workaholics."

He laughed. "I've noticed that."

They returned their empty glasses to Andrea and said goodbye, then packed his tools in the truck. He turned to Callie.

"Thanks for your help. You're a real trooper."

"Yep. Just call me Bob the Builder." She laughed.

He grinned. "Tomorrow afternoon, when you get off work?"

"After lunch."

"Sounds good." His voice sounded tired and soft. She suddenly wondered what it would be like to be his wife, to hear him at the end of the day, to feel his arms around her.

"Callie?"

"Yeah?" she said, forcing her eyes to focus on him.

"You're standing in front of my car door."

"Oh, sorry." Thankful for the darkness, she stepped aside. A crimson face didn't suit her. Especially when she wore rust nail polish.

"No problem. But I don't think you'd want to stay right here. I'm sure you've smelled better."

Let me be the judge of that.

"Good night, Brad," she said.

"Good night." He opened his door. Once she'd settled into her car and started the engine, he waved and eased onto the road.

He'd make a nice husband for a woman willing to travel the globe.

Chapter Fifteen

The last appointment on Callie's schedule canceled, so she stopped by the nursing home to check on Gram before going to work on the playhouse. Usually, she could hear Gram teasing the nurses or residents, but lately when Callie'd stopped by, she was sleeping. Callie hoped to find Gram's energy up today.

"Who is it?"

"It's me, Gram. Callie."

Gram extended her bony arm. "Oh, come here, sweet Callie."

She crossed the distance between them and grabbed Gram's hand. The old woman looked more feeble every day. Callie brushed a strand of hair from Gram's cheek.

"You keeping up with your meals?"

"Have you seen what they try to feed me?" Gram whispered.

Callie laughed. "Can't be that bad."

Gram waved her hand. "Worse."

"How about I check with the staff and see if I can bring you in something."

Gram's eyes lit up as though she'd just been granted twenty extra years by her fairy godmother.

"Well, bring it on, honey," she said with a weak chuckle. "That cake you brought in was to die for—" Gram cleared her throat "—um, so to speak."

Callie laughed. "Okay, next week I'll bring dinner."

"Now that the house is built, Brad will be itchin' to leave," Gram said, plunging right into what was obviously on her heart.

Shadows darkened corners and cast a haze over the room. Callie opened the blinds, allowing the evening sun to fill the room with light.

"Is that too much?" Callie asked.

"No, dear. It's just fine. Come sit by me."

Callie slipped into the chair by the bed and held Gram's hand.

"You love him, don't you?"

Callie's breath caught in her throat and threatened to stay there. "Who?"

"I think you know." Gram patted her hand and lifted a weak smile.

"We're just friends."

Gram raised a brow. "I guess they've changed the meaning of *friends* these days." She turned liquid eyes to Callie. "You need to let him know. Before he goes."

"He has to go where his heart leads him."

"I know that boy as well as my own self, and his heart is with you. I've never seen him light up like that when anyone else is around. And he's dated plenty, mark my words." Gram straightened the sheet around her. "Some of them scared me half to death."

Callie laughed. "Gram, you're something else."

"Just think about what I said."

"Okay, I'll think about it," Callie said, knowing she wouldn't be able to think of anything else.

The sun had long since slipped from the horizon. The plywood floor and much of the walls had been constructed for the playhouse. Every bone in Callie's body ached. She rolled her head from side to side.

"It's time to call it a night," Brad said.

It was all she could do not to sprint off the job to a hot bath. Instead, she helped Brad pack up.

"Want to meet here on Monday? We could grab a sandwich after work and head on over here," Brad said, packing the hammer in his toolbox.

"Yeah, that would work. I'm not sure when my last appointment is, but I'll call and let you know."

"That would be great." He stood up and let out a slight groan, his hand grasping his back. When he caught her looking at him, he said, "Guess I'm getting old."

She smiled. "I know the feeling."

They'd been quiet for a moment, looking at their work, when Brad said, "I still miss her."

He didn't have to say who. Callie knew.

"I'm sorry, Brad."

He ran his hand through his hair. "No, I'm sorry. It's just that the playhouse—well, when we were kids, Nicole had a playhouse. Anytime it lost a nail or needed a coat of paint, she turned to me." He laughed. "Guess I was destined to be a carpenter."

Callie smiled. "You're a natural, that's for sure."

"I shouldn't have left her. She'd always been so frail, you know?" Brad's gaze traveled to Callie, as though searching for support.

"Yes, she was frail. But you couldn't have known what would happen, Brad."

"I'm sorry I blamed you when I first found out you knew her. Guess I was just so upset that someone didn't notice her problem, like that jerk husband of hers."

"People make choices, and we have no control over that." Callie could tell he was trying to control his breathing. Nicole's death haunted him daily. If only Callie could help him. She took his hand, causing him to look up at her. "Sometimes, you've just got to let it go."

"Is that what you've done? With your dad, I mean?" His question probed Callie's heart with painful intensity.

"I'm working on it," she finally whispered.

He squeezed her hard. "We'll get there one day."

"Yeah," was the only thing she said, praying with all her heart it was so, and noticing how nice it felt to hold Brad Sharp's hand.

Chaos stumbled over the fluffy comforter on Callie's bed as they settled in for the night. He snuggled into Callie, the clean scent of shampoo coming off him. The tags on his collar jingled as she scratched his long, floppy ears. He brought her such joy that she wondered how she could ever let him go. Still, visions of Chaos and Micah romping together crowded her mind. Was she being selfish to keep him?

She thought back to what Heather had said about Chaos when they'd been talking about her dad. Of course, Callie wasn't a puppy, but sometimes she wondered if her dad had felt the same way about her. Maybe he thought she was better off staying with Aunt Bonnie and Uncle George than with him. Obviously, she would never know.

Chaos circled three times and finally fell in a heap at the foot of the bed. Callie reached over to turn on her music and glanced at the Bible on her nightstand, an old friend with whom she had lost touch. It seemed that the more consumed she became with her father's abandonment, the more she avoided her Heavenly Father. She remembered how she had felt rejected by everyone—including God—at that point in her life. As an adult, of course, she knew better.

She gingerly picked up the Bible, hoping and praying God would give her something, anything, to let her know He had not forgotten her. When she picked up the leather book and flipped through it, a small laminated card fell from the pages. Aunt Bonnie had given it to her long ago. The card showed a little girl kneeling in the middle of a large hand. Across the top was an excerpt from Isaiah.

"Can a mother forget the baby at her breast and have no compassion on the child she has borne? Though she may forget, I will not forget you. See, I have engraved you on the palms of my hands."

Callie read the words with disbelief. How had she overlooked it for so long? Why had she? She knew it was no accident that she read the words now. Tears slid down her face with the knowledge of God's agape love that would not let her go. A love that understood her pain and walked her through it—if she would accept it.

She slid out of bed and knelt down by the floor. Chaos came over to her and nudged her hand.

"Why can't I let this go, Lord? I'm a grown woman. Dad chose to walk away. Why can't I just accept that?"

Hot tears of guilt and blame flowed. She knew all her questions would not be answered at once, but with her prayer came the knowing that she would get through the days ahead—without her dad—because her Heavenly Father was there. Always had been. Always would be.

Callie didn't know what the future held. She could no longer deny the love in her heart for Brad. He was out of reach, and she would just have to accept that—the way she had to accept that her father was gone and would never come back. One thing she'd learned from it all, though. She could never abandon family the way he did. He had made his choice, and she was making hers.

She would live and die in Burrow, Ohio.

* * *

"Hey, Callie, we'll have to call off working on the playhouse tonight," Brad said, pacing his kitchen. "Gram has taken a turn for the worse, and they've called in the family."

"Oh, no! I'm so sorry, Brad," Callie said.

"Would you pray for her—for us? She's such a great lady and I don't want her to suffer."

"I would be honored to pray, Brad."

"Thanks. I'll keep you posted." He clicked off. Just knowing Callie was praying gave him comfort.

He picked up his mom and they hurried over to see Gram.

"You gonna be all right, Mom?" Brad asked as they stood just outside the entrance of the nursing home. His eyes searched hers. "I mean, if Gram—"

She put her hand on his arm. "I'll be fine, Brad. I've known this day was coming, I just didn't know when. We'll make it through, no matter what."

He nodded and took a deep breath. He pulled her arm through his. "Let's go."

Brad could not believe what they saw when they entered the room. Instead of Gram breathing her last breath, she was sitting up and laughing with an attendant.

"Well, don't just stand there with your mouths

hanging open, get over here and give me a hug," Gram said with a twinkle in her eyes.

Amid tears and laughter, Brad and Annie hugged Gram. She said in her no-nonsense fashion, "What's the matter? Did you have me written off already? It ain't over till the old lady sings, remember?"

"Only you, Gram. Only you." Brad shook his head and chuckled.

"So, what happened?" Annie asked.

Gram shrugged. "Oh, same old thing. This old ticker is giving out on me. One day you'll come in here and I really will be gone, but in the meantime, I'm still kickin'. Come here, you two, there's something I want to talk to you about."

Annie walked over and sat on the bed. Brad stood beside them.

"I've been wondering why people wait until they're dead to dole out their gifts to their loved ones. I know I need to keep some money back for my living expenses, but I have plenty to part with, too."

Brad and Annie exchanged a glance.

"Surprised?" She chuckled. "The truth is, I'm rich. Have been for years. But I've never been one to live high on the hog. It just ain't in me. I've given my share to charities, but I wanted to save some for my family. Annie, my boy is gone, but you've been just like a daughter to me from the day you married into our family. I don't believe Naomi loved Ruth any more than I love you. I hope I can live long enough to see you put this to good use." Gram handed her a check.

Annie held up her palm. "Mom, don't do this. You've been through a lot, and you need time to think about this. It's a major decision."

"Now, Annie, don't you be stubborn about this. My mind's made up."

"How does your attorney feel about it?" Annie said.

"Ain't none of his business. It's my money. I can do what I want with it. And yes, I'm still of sound mind. Just had a couple of witnesses here at the nursing home sign a paper swearing to it."

"Were they residents?" Brad asked with a laugh.

Gram let out a hearty whoop. "No, they weren't. I may be old, but I'm not stupid."

Annie reluctantly took the check, appearing very unsettled about the whole thing. When Annie glanced at it, her eyes widened and she shook her head. "My goodness, no, Mom! You may need this money to take care of yourself. Where on earth did you get all this?"

"Your father-in-law wasn't the only one who played the stocks," she said with a glint in her eyes.

Annie's jaw dropped.

"Gram, you been holding out on us?" Brad was happy for his mom. She could use a boost to encourage her spirits. Maybe there would be enough for her to take a trip or buy something she'd always wanted.

"A girl's gotta have something up her sleeve every now and then. I didn't forget you, either, Brad, my boy."

"Gram—" Brad began.

She cut him off. "Now, don't you start, too. This is an old lady's dying wishes. Now you take it."

"You don't look like you're dying to me," he teased.

Her gnarled thumb and index finger thumped against her chest. She laid her head against the pillow with great drama. "Got a bad ticker."

"Don't count on any academy awards." Brad grinned.

Gram popped her head up. "I can take this back, you know." She shoved the check into his hand. "Here, now take it."

"Thanks, Gram."

"Well, don't be mannerly about it. You know you're dying to see how much it is. So do it while I can see ya." Her eyes studied him carefully.

Brad turned the check over and when he saw the amount on the check, he started coughing.

She smiled and thumped back against her bed with obvious satisfaction.

"Gram, I don't—you don't—"

She waved her hand. "Just say thank you and be done with it." Her face beamed.

"Thank you." He kissed her. "I love you, Gram—and it has nothing to do with the money."

She smiled and piped up, "But it sure helps." She chuckled and handed him an envelope.

He turned the envelope over in his hands. "What's this one for?"

"For Callie." She pointed at him. "And don't you question it. It's my money to dispose of as I please."

"Wasn't going to, Gram. I quite agree with you."

She smiled. "I thought you would. See that she gets it, will you?"

"I will."

"Now you can use that money to fund your way through mission work overseas or do something with it right here. The choice is yours. Just make sure of one thing," she said.

"What's that?" Brad asked.

She sat up a moment and looked him square in the eyes. "You make sure whatever choice you make, you make it for the right reasons." She sank back into her pillow. "Now, go celebrate your day. I need a nap."

Chapter Sixteen

"But I don't understand. Why would she give this to me?" Callie stared at the envelope. As much as she appreciated Gram's gesture, she didn't feel right about taking it.

Brad shrugged. "I guess she likes the way you fix her hair." He winked. "Besides, you should know Gram well enough to know that not everyone can win her over."

Callie nibbled at her lower lip. "I just don't know."

Brad dropped the nails back into his toolbox and covered her hand. "She wants you to have it, Callie, or she wouldn't have given it to you. Make an old woman happy and just accept it." He took the envelope back from her and stuffed it in her bag.

With her luck, it would be lost forever.

She wanted to change the subject. "How do

you feel about classical music?" Her question caused him to make a face.

"Where did that come from?" He laughed.

"The Philharmonic is giving a concert in a few weeks, and I can get tickets." Did she just ask him on a date? Being desperate to change the subject was one thing, but why did she have to do that?

He held up his hand. "No offense to you, but there are two things I don't do—cook and go to orchestra-type concerts. Just not my thing." He dropped his measuring tool and stood to face her. "I prefer those high-energy, hand-clapping, feet-stomping kind of concerts."

She should have stayed on the subject of Gram's money.

"But I would love to get together with you." He took a step toward her. "Now, would you rather talk about Gram's money?" A teasing glint lit his eyes.

She took a step back. "I just don't want anyone to think—"

He took a step closer. "Think what?" His gaze probed deeply into hers, as though searching her heart with a spotlight.

Another step back. "That I—"

"I don't think anything other than you've captured Gram's heart just like you've captured—" her breath caught in her throat, making an audible sound "—Mom's heart…and…the Sauderses'."

Disappointment ran through her, but it was ridiculous, of course. What had she expected him to say? He kept his eyes on her, neither one of them daring to make so much as a twitch. The hearts with fluttering wings were back—and they'd brought friends.

"It seems you have that effect on people." He reached his hand down to her hair and lifted a strand as though testing the softness of a silky scarf. His head dipped toward hers. Their lips melted together. Emotions swirled and tangled with reason. Callie knew she had to let him go. If he wanted to leave Burrow, she shouldn't hold him here. He would always blame her. With great reluctance, she broke free from the strong embrace of his arms, the warmth of his breath upon her lips, the brush of his whiskers against her face.

Weakness tingled down her arms and legs. Her breath came in shallow puffs.

"Gram gave me a gift, too," he said.

Callie's stomach clenched and her throat tightened. "So when will you be leaving?" She tried to make her tone cheerful, though an ache clutched her heart and refused to let go.

"I haven't been asked to go on assignment anywhere," he said.

"Not yet. But if the opportunity presents itself,

you'll go," she said, trying desperately to hide the plea in her voice for him stay.

His hand reached under her chin, forcing her to look at him. "Look, Callie, I—" The pain in his eyes was more than she could bear. It was too much to ask, and she knew it. If he thought he should serve elsewhere, she had no right to ask him to do otherwise.

She pulled away from him. "It's getting late. I really need to go. I'll be sure and thank Gram." She steadied herself, making her way over wood slats and cords.

"You'll be back?"

The sound of his voice curled around her heart. She turned to him.

"To help me finish the playhouse…I mean."

With sheer determination she pulled a smile into place. "Yes, of course I'll help you finish the playhouse. Good night." Satisfied that her words sounded pleasant enough, she waved over her shoulder and headed toward her car. Tears threatened, but she steeled herself against them. She thought of Gram's advice and wondered if it would change things if she told Brad how she really felt. But of course she couldn't do that. She wouldn't hold him back from his dream. People had left her before and she'd survived.

She could do it again.

* * *

Callie had just settled into bed when the phone rang.

"You didn't give me a chance to finish what I was going to say," Brad said before she could even say hello.

"Okay, what were you going to say?" Callie wasn't sure she wanted to hear this, but it didn't appear she had a choice.

"I was going to tell you that I've been offered a job—"

"Oh." Her spirits plummeted.

"—here in Burrow."

Hope surged but skepticism kept it in check. "Doing what?"

He explained about the offer his brother had presented to him.

"But I thought you wanted to work in another country?"

"I did, too."

"And now?"

He let out a long sigh. "I'm not sure."

She didn't know if that answer had a double meaning. Maybe his feelings for her were growing. There was an obvious attraction between them, but was it a surface relationship on his part, or did his caring go deeper than that? Should she tell him how she felt? Propriety told her it wasn't her place to do that. Shouldn't he be the one to express himself to her first?

"Well, I'll be praying for you, Brad. I know it's a big decision."

"Yeah. For more reasons than you might think."

Hope shot through her. Should she dare ask him why or just revel in the possibilities? Before she could decide, he thanked her for her prayer support and told her he had to go.

For the first time ever she would allow herself to dream of a future with Brad Sharp.

Callie crossed the kitchen to grab her handbag and keys. Her body begged for coffee after a night of bad sleep. She'd tossed and turned, trying to figure out exactly what Brad had meant.

No matter what happened between them, God would give her the strength she needed, because she trusted in Him. That didn't mean the path would be easy. She wasn't that naive. Life was hard, but God was always good. He'd get her through it.

She grabbed her bag and her gaze fell on the envelope from Gram. In all the commotion of last night, she had completely forgotten about it. Her fingers ripped through the envelope flap and lifted out a check, the amount of which made her falter a moment. In her hands was enough money to assure her aunt and uncle a memorable anniversary. This money would relieve her of the extra pressure of working so many hours. It was a gift she didn't deserve, but for some reason Gram wanted her to have it. Why? Gram hardly knew her.

When Callie's cell phone rang, it startled her. A glance at the clock told her it was Heather. She anxiously flipped open the phone as she headed out the door.

They exchanged their morning greetings and Callie got down to business, telling Heather about last night and Gram's gift.

Heather let out a whistle. "That is a nice gift."

"Do you think I should accept it?" Callie settled into her car and edged onto the street.

"Well, of course you should. She wanted you to have it or she wouldn't have given it to you. You must have made quite an impression on her."

"Honestly, Heather, I think she believes I will be a member of the family and that's why she gave me the money."

"Well, sometimes older people have a sense about these things."

Callie almost didn't notice when the stoplight turned green. "That could be, but I don't know."

"Does he still want to go to South America?"

"I don't know." Callie decided not to say

anything about Brad's job offer. She didn't want to raise false hopes. They'd have to wait and see what happened.

Heather hit her horn. "That guy cut right in front of me!"

"You okay?" Heather wasn't known for her patience.

"Yes. I hate it when people do that." She paused. "So, do you think Brad is running from something here in Burrow?"

"Yeah, I think he is."

"His sister's death?"

"That would be my guess."

"Hmm, you may be onto something. I know Judge Sharp has expressed a concern for his little brother. Still, lots of people move away from their hometown."

"Yeah, you're right. Maybe I'm looking for something to blame it on, wishing I were enough of a reason for him to stay."

"So you admit it?"

"Admit what?"

"That you're in love with Brad?"

She hadn't meant to confess that. Somehow saying it out loud to another person made her feel vulnerable and exposed. But there was no going back now. Heather knew her too well.

"Yeah, I guess I do."

"I'll be praying for you, Callie. Things will work out, you'll see."

"Doesn't always work out the way we want," Callie said.

"I know. But you'll get through it."

"Yeah." *I always do.*

Brad's body ached. He'd been pushing hard to get the playhouse done in time for Micah's returned. Callie had turned out to be more of a distraction than a help. It wasn't her fault. He couldn't seem to keep his mind on the work when she was around. He'd asked her to help, though, so he could hardly tell her to stop coming around now.

He had a little time before she would join him so he decided to do something he hadn't done before. He pulled into the gated cemetery where Nicole was laid to rest.

Sunlight dappled the sycamores, and birds sang a soothing melody. He thought it interesting that cemeteries were so peaceful even the birds cooperated. When he reached Nicole's grave, he was surprised to see a vase of daisies. He didn't think his mom would have visited. Though she had been feeling much better these days, he didn't think she would have been in the frame of mind to come visit the grave just yet. It could have been

Ryan, though he couldn't see Ryan doing something like this. He was too methodical about life. Not that he wasn't compassionate, but life was what it was, and he saw little need for all the frivolities that accompanied emotion.

Whether his mom or Ryan, it didn't matter. Somehow the flowers comforted him. Maybe because he thought they would please Nicole. He should have thought of it himself. But the fact was he hadn't been here to visit before. It shamed him to think he hadn't come, but he couldn't bring himself to face the truth before now. Yes, he knew she had died, but seeing the grave marker with her name and dates on it made it seem so…so…final.

The air around him barely stirred as he whispered his grief to his sister. A tear spilled down his face while he uttered his regrets and apologies for not being there for her. Growing up together, they had shared their dreams of the future. They had given one another advice about love interests, and now he brought to her his love for Callie. It seemed only fitting that he tell his sister about the woman who had stolen his heart. From there, his thoughts went to Ryan's offer. He hadn't prayed about it and he'd said he would. It's not that he didn't want to pray. He knew God could use him anywhere. Even in Burrow. Yet, working in other countries had always seemed the right thing to do.

Still, as the words poured from his soul, he surrendered his future to God's leading. He could work in Burrow or elsewhere. He'd leave the decision to God and be obedient—no matter the path ahead of him.

Callie was right about something else, too. He had been running from guilt over Nicole. But he had been wrong. It wasn't his fault. He could see that now. Still, his heart grieved for the loss of his sister.

Once he pulled his car onto the street, Brad had settled something deep inside his heart. He would pray about his decision, and come next week, if he still felt sure in his heart that this was the right thing to do, he would let Ryan know his decision one way or the other.

He didn't know what the future held, but wherever it took him, he hoped and prayed Callie Easton would be a part of it.

"What's this for?" Bonnie asked when Callie handed her the vase of red roses.

"Because I love you." Callie kissed her on the cheek. "And because I feel bad I haven't had time to spend with you lately. I've been so wrapped up in work and helping with that playhouse."

"Oh, honey, you didn't need to do this. I know you've been busy." She took a whiff of the fragrant petals. "These are lovely." She gave Callie a sideways squeeze. "Thank you." Walking over to her manicure station, Aunt Bonnie rearranged some polish bottles and placed her vase there.

"How's Uncle George?" Callie asked, preparing her hair station for her next client.

Bonnie ran a dust cloth across a shelf. "Oh, you know your uncle. Same old, same old." She chuckled. "He's been playing those video games every night. I'm just about ready to pull the plug on him."

Callie laughed. "He's fifty-six going on sixteen."

"Exactly," Bonnie shifted hair product around on the shelf.

"Which reminds me, you've got an anniversary coming up. How many years is it now?"

"Thirty-five, can you believe it?" Bonnie said, wistfully.

Callie shook her head.

"Did I ever tell you that your dad set us up?" She smiled. "My brother was always looking out for me." The moment she said it, she appeared to regret it. They both knew why. He certainly hadn't looked out for Callie.

Callie didn't comment on that. "So, what would you think of a little party for your anniversary?"

The words barely left Callie's mouth before

Bonnie shook her head. "George and I don't enjoy parties. You know we like things low-key." She shrugged. "That's just us. A quiet dinner out, now, that sounds perfect," Bonnie said. "We've never been fans of all the hubbub."

Callie smiled. "I know." But of course that wouldn't stop her from planning…something.

Callie had planted colorful petunias in the window box of the playhouse along with vines that spilled over the wooden edge. Brad had put a small shrub on either side of the front entrance. They stood back and admired their project, knowing Micah would be there any minute. Callie clapped her hands together. "It is beautiful, Brad. Thank you so much for letting me be a part of it."

He studied her. The joy on her face warmed him clear through. On impulse he grabbed her close and gave her a hug. "This is our gift to Micah." He smiled down at her, and his heart took a leap in his chest. He couldn't help thinking he was staring into the eyes of his soul mate. Yet there were so many questions, so many uncertainties about the future. He wanted to stay in Burrow now, but was he letting his love for her get in the way of rational decision making? Before he could think more on that, Callie reached up and kissed him softly on the lips.

"Thank you." She quickly turned away, leaving him speechless, his heart thrumming wildly within him.

"Here we go," Mick Sauders announced, causing them both to turn with a start. Andrea put her finger to her lips as they came around the corner so Brad and Callie wouldn't say anything and spoil the surprise.

The family walked toward them. A blindfold was wrapped around Micah's eyes. Mick guided her footsteps, directing her toward the playhouse. She giggled with every step.

"What is it, Daddy?"

The grown-ups smiled, each one as excited as the child.

"Is Chaos out here, Mommy?"

Brad noticed the flicker of a shadow in Callie's eyes.

"No, honey, Chaos is not here."

"Oh," she said, disappointed.

"Are you ready?" Mick asked.

"Ready!" Micah shouted with a sharp nod of her head.

"Okay, here we go." He unwrapped the blindfold and everyone shouted, "Surprise!"

Micah's eyes grew large as walnuts. Her mouth dropped but not a single utterance spilled out. She walked over to the little pink cottage, stepped up to the porch and ran her fingers along the wooden columns as though they were gold. She looked in disbelief first to her parents, then to Brad and Callie. "Is this—mine?" Apprehension lined her question, as though merely saying it would wake her up from a beautiful dream.

"Yes, honey, this is yours," Brad said.

Micah ran over to Brad and Callie and hugged them furiously. Then Andrea took Micah into the house so she could collect her treasured dolls and serve them tea in the new playhouse. Brad had never known a more perfect day in his entire life. He studied Callie's face as she watched Micah play, more convinced than ever that staying in Burrow was the right decision.

Now all he had to do was tell her.

Chapter Seventeen

When Callie got home from work the following Friday, she noticed Chaos seemed a bit lethargic. She'd fed him, but he just didn't seem himself. If he kept acting that way, she'd take him to see the vet in the morning.

Right after dinner, Chaos sat by the back door and whined, a sure sign he needed to go outside. After letting him out, her doorbell rang. She wondered if it might be Brad with bad news. Before opening the door, she braced herself.

She was surprised to find Andrea and Micah. Though Callie had given them an open invitation to visit Chaos, they had never come before.

"Well, hello. Come on in." Callie stepped aside so they could enter.

After settling on the sofa, Andrea started to tell

why they had come to visit when Chaos barked from outside.

Micah perked up, but her mother laid a calming hand on Micah's knee.

No sooner had Callie opened the back door than Chaos went romping through the kitchen and into the living room. She watched with disbelief as life sparked through him and he jumped on a giggling Micah.

"Are you all right?" Andrea asked, studying Callie.

"Yes, I'm—I'm fine." Callie sat, her gaze never leaving Chaos. "It's just that he didn't seem— well, earlier he seemed—oh, never mind. It doesn't matter now." She lifted a smile to Andrea, trying to hide the dull ache in her heart.

"Micah begged me to see if you would allow Chaos to spend the night with us." While the puppy and little girl played together, Andrea leaned in to Callie. "Micah thinks Chaos is a little friend."

Callie grinned. "I can see that." After a moment of watching the two together, Callie said, "Sure, I don't see why Chaos can't go. The nice thing about dogs is I don't have to pack an overnight bag."

After a while Andrea and Micah walked out of the house with Chaos in tow. Callie waved goodbye with sadness in her heart.

She knew what she had to do. The question was when.

After Chaos left with the Sauders, Callie decided she couldn't stay home. She grabbed her keys and handbag and headed out the door. The smell of early summer scented the air. Twilight had settled over Burrow. Pulling her car into the cemetery lot, Callie got out and strolled over to the familiar place she had come to visit so many times before.

She and Nicole had not been best friends. Still, somehow she could talk to Nicole about Brad in ways she couldn't to anyone else—not even Heather or Aunt Bonnie.

When she got there, she placed a fresh vase of daisies by the headstone and took the other one away. She'd take it home and clean it out, then refill it and bring it back. She hoped the family wouldn't mind what she was doing. But then how would they know? No doubt they grieved too much to visit.

She settled into the portable cloth chair she brought with her each time she visited. Wrapped in birdsong and twilight, Callie recorded her thoughts in a journal, stopping occasionally to talk to Nicole.

Twilight melted into night and peace replaced her fears of the future, one pen stroke at a time.

"Would you repeat that, Mark?" Brad asked. "The line cut out just as you said that."

Mark Huston, a fellow missionary and friend said, "We want you to come over and head up our building project here in Belize."

"Belize." Just when Brad thought he had settled the matter in his mind.

"Yep."

Brad could hear the smile in his friend's voice. Normally, he would be jumping up and down for joy. Everything was a go. He had the money, he had the time and now he had the opportunity. But one thing stood in his way.

Callie.

"Wow, that's quite an offer."

"We don't know of a better man for the job than you, Brad. You are gifted, bro."

"Thanks."

"Do I hear some hesitation?" Mark asked with concern.

"Well, you know, I want to pray about it. Make sure I do the right thing."

"Sure, of course. Too bad you can't come over here and take a look. That might help you decide."

This was a huge decision. It could change the course of his life forever.

"That's a good idea. I'll come for a visit, then make my decision."

"Well, that would be great." His friend was practically breathless with excitement, telling him all that he would show him—the people, the needs, the work to be done. By the end of the conversation they had come to a decision that Brad would leave as soon as he could get a reasonable ticket.

When Brad hung up the phone, he was more confused than ever. Just when he thought he had made up his mind to stay in Burrow, this came up.

He glanced at the ceiling. "Are you messin' with me, Lord?" He grabbed his keys and went to the one place he could not only talk to the Lord but also talk things over with the only best friend he'd ever had.

Nicole.

Callie glanced up at the sky, finished the last sentence in her journal and closed it. She hadn't realized it had gotten so late. "Thanks for listening to me," she whispered.

Just then she heard a twig snap. She whipped around.

"So you're the one." Brad stepped into view in the moonlight.

"Oh, uh, the one what?" She stood and closed her chair, wanting desperately to make a hasty retreat.

"The one who brought the daisies for Nicole. I should have known."

"Is that all right?"

"Only you would think of such a thing. Thanks."

"You're welcome. I didn't think you came here. I knew the grief was so great…" She let the words trail off.

He gazed at the grave. "You're right. I couldn't bring myself to come here. Until recently." He looked back to Callie. "Sounds kind of crazy, but I like to talk to her."

"I know. Me, too." She hoped he was talking to Nicole about the possibility of staying in Burrow. Maybe this was a good sign. Though deep down she wished he'd talk to her about it.

Something about him tonight looked off-kilter. "You all right?" she asked.

"Sure, I'm fine." He cleared his throat. "I'm taking a trip to Belize in a couple of days," he said as though he were taking a trip across town. No big deal.

"Oh, sounds nice. How long will you be gone?" A sick ball of worry formed in her stomach, its tendrils reaching up through her chest to her throat, causing it to constrict.

"I'm not sure. I'm checking it out." He hesitated. "They've offered me a job there, to oversee home construction."

Her stomach clenched. "Oh, really?" She tried to appear happy about the news, to share his joy, regardless of whether it rocked her world.

"It's beautiful country. You should see it."

"I don't have the need to see the world the way you do."

"Callie, wait, before you get all—"

"Look, Brad, you don't have to explain to me. If that's what you feel you should do, I say go for it. You've made it clear from day one that that was your dream, so follow it. You don't have anything in Burrow to hold you here. Your mom is doing better and so is Gram. Besides, your brother can take care of them, and you have your own life to live. Hope it's a great one." She tromped off the premises, leaving him speechless.

There. She'd done it. Rejected him before he could reject her.

By the time she got to the car, her hands were shaking and tears pooled in her eyes. But she would not cry. Not this time.

After dinner Callie, Aunt Bonnie and Uncle George settled into the living room.

"Your hair looks nice. I was surprised to see you changed it back to blonde so soon," Aunt Bonnie said.

Callie shrugged. "I like blonde better."

They both knew it was more than that.

"Have you heard from him?" Aunt Bonnie asked before sipping from her teacup.

Callie shook her head and studied her nail polish. She hadn't worn pink pearl or coral in a while.

"Should be home soon. What's it been, a week?" Aunt Bonnie asked.

Callie nodded. "I don't know how long he's staying. Maybe he'll make the decision to just stay there."

"I doubt that. You don't know for sure that he's even accepting the job, right?"

"He will. It's everything he's been wanting."

Aunt Bonnie sighed. "I can't help feeling responsible. I encouraged you to—to—"

"To what, Bonnie? Hunt the poor man down till he agreed to walk down the aisle?" Uncle George tsked-tsked. "You women and your matchmaking. Don't you listen to her, Beanie," he said. "If God wants you together, you'll be together. If not, you're better off without him."

Aunt Bonnie shrugged. "You're right, and I was wrong."

"Stop the presses! The woman admits she's wrong."

"Oh, you," Bonnie said.

Callie looked at her aunt and uncle, and a fresh wave of love washed over her, reminding her once again why she couldn't leave Burrow. As much as she loved Brad, she could not leave them.

"Well, it sounds as though Brad has some exciting possibilities," Uncle George said.

"I suppose," Callie said. "Though I don't know how he could leave Burrow."

Aunt Bonnie studied her. "We have to follow God's call upon our hearts, wherever that may lead us."

Callie looked at her. "I could never leave Burrow. You and Uncle George are my family."

"And you think God needs you to look after us?"

"Well—"

"He's quite capable of handling us, you know."

She hated it when Aunt Bonnie put a spin on things this way. "I know, but—"

"We know where your allegiance lies, Callie. We know you would never leave us out of a selfish heart. We also know that if God asked you to leave, you would be obedient. We would expect nothing less from you."

Callie heard the strong words and struggled with the idea that God would ever take her away from Burrow.

As she drove home, Aunt Bonnie's words haunted her, though she'd tried her best to push them away. Aunt Bonnie was giving her blessing, and so was Uncle George, to go, if need be.

Letting go. That was love. Real love. Agape

love. Could she let go of Brad? Aunt Bonnie and Uncle George?

She stumbled in through the door of her bedroom and flopped onto her bed. Chaos whined to get out of his crate.

Instantly, Callie saw herself as she was. Selfish. From head to toe. Wanting Brad for herself. Wanting Chaos though she knew he would be better off with Micah. True love didn't choke. True love allowed people to dream. It encouraged people to be their best. Giving them the freedom to be who they were. Fear of rejection caused Callie to hang on too tight or walk away completely, to keep from getting hurt.

Callie took a long, deep breath, then looked at Chaos. "I'm going to do this before I lose my nerve." Grabbing his leash, crate and food and water bowls, Callie placed them in the car. "Come on, Chaos. Go bye-bye." The spaniel pup jumped into the travel carrier and she strapped it in.

Though her heart ached, the thought of Micah's face gave her the courage to do what she thought she could never do—give Chaos to the family who could offer him more of something than she ever could.

Time.

Palm trees waved with the night breeze. Brad drank in the sea air. The waters raced to shore, depositing seaweed and shells, then rushed back to sea to pick up more. This was Brad's last night in Belize, and he still wasn't sure what to do. His enthusiasm had definitely waned from prior months, but he didn't want anyone to keep him from fulfilling God's plan for his life, whatever that might be.

Stars shone in a clear sky. He climbed a large boulder and stared out to sea. If only he could share this with Callie. He glanced back at the forest thick with green foliage. Exotic parrots and toucans fluttered in the trees. His gaze wandered to a thatch-roofed open shelter complete with hammocks that called residents to a gentle rest in the trade winds. Palm and coconut trees clustered inland, while tropical flowers of bright reds, yellows, oranges and pinks sprinkled color across the land. The distant Maya Mountains offered adventures for another day.

All these things normally called to him in a way he couldn't explain to another human being. The very thought of them had stirred a passion, a longing, inside him that nothing else—or no one else—could satisfy. Until now.

Though he still admired the beauty of this paradise, it didn't hold the same lure it once had. The pull of helping others grew stronger every day, but this visit confirmed what his spirit would never consider before. He didn't have to serve here to use the gifts God had given to him. He merely had to do the best he could, with the gifts he had, wherever life took him.

"Mind if I join you?" Mark walked up beside him.

"Feel free," Brad said, scooting over on the boulder.

"It's beautiful here, isn't it?" Mark said, dumping sand from his shoes.

"Amazing."

"You know, Brad, it doesn't mean you are failing God if you don't come here. You can make a difference anywhere."

Brad turned to him. "Why are you saying that?" He could hardly believe Mark had said the very words he had been thinking.

Mark shrugged and threw a pebble out to sea. "There's something that's not quite right about all this."

"You don't think I'm a good fit?"

"It's not that you're not a good fit, but I'm not convinced you're the one who's supposed to come."

"Thanks a lot."

Mark laughed and slapped his friend good-naturedly on the back. "I'm not making your decision for you. I'm just saying God may have other plans for you. You're equipped to do the work here, no doubt about it, but you seem a little restless, man."

Brad nodded. "I know."

"Be open, buddy. Who knows where the Lord will lead you."

"What if it's to Burrow?"

Mark shrugged again. "There is no place you'd rather be than in the center of God's will, bro."

"Yeah, but how do you know if it's God's will or your own will disguising itself to get you to do what you want?"

"That's a tough one. You're the only one who can answer that. But you know if you've found a good woman who loves Him, too, you can do His work anywhere. You have gifts in carpentry, no question about it. You can use that gift in helping with your church, building homes for the poor, whatever. But you have other gifts to offer, too, Brad. Compassion is your biggest gift. That's needed everywhere. Even in Burrow."

He nodded.

"Maybe you'll work abroad later."

Brad shook his head. "Callie would never leave Burrow."

"One thing I've learned where God is concerned—never say 'never.' If she truly loves God, she'll follow where He leads." Mark squeezed his buddy's shoulder. "I'll be praying for you." He got up and walked back to his house, leaving Brad staring at the sea.

Chapter Eighteen

Callie backed the car out of her garage and headed down the road, willing herself to be strong. But Chaos was *her* dog—she didn't have to give him away. He was happy with her. He didn't know any better.

But when visions of Chaos and Micah came to her mind, she knew without a doubt she was doing the right thing.

On the drive over to the Sauderses' home, Callie's thoughts traveled to Brad. Was he having a good time? Had he already committed to staying there? Would she ever see him again? A vise strangled her heart. She couldn't go there. Not now. She was giving up her dog and most likely the one man she loved all at the same time. A tear slipped down her cheek and she brushed it away.

She pulled into the driveway, and Andrea ran outside to meet her.

"You're sure about this, Callie?" Worry lines deepened between her brows.

"I'm sure. Are you? I mean, maybe my call caught you off guard. You don't have to take him. It's totally up to you."

Andrea smiled. "Micah loves him so much. All she talks about is Chaos this and Chaos that." She laughed. "We welcome him into our family."

Chaos barked and shuffled around in his carrier. The two women laughed.

"I guess he's ready." She smiled to disguise the struggle inside her.

"Micah is reading in her room. I'll call her out and we can surprise her." Excitement shone from Andrea's eyes. She turned to leave, then swung back around to face Callie. "Thank you." She gave her a quick hug, then headed toward the house.

Once Andrea disappeared from view, Callie took Chaos out of his carrier and knelt down in front of him. "It sure didn't take you long to wrap yourself around my heart." She scratched behind his floppy ears and nuzzled into him. "I'll miss you." After a moment she stood up. "Let's go."

Callie tugged on his leash and Chaos trotted along happily beside her. They stepped quietly into the house. Chaos padded excitedly around her. "Stay still," Callie whispered. Chaos settled at her feet.

A door opened and footsteps approached from the hallway. Chaos's ears perked and he stood. He let out a whine and his paws clacked against the hardwood in the entryway.

"Who's here?" Micah asked her mother just as they rounded the corner. Her face broke into a smile when she saw Chaos. She ran to him and threw her arms around him. Andrea and Callie laughed as they watched a tangle of arms and paws roll around on the living room floor.

"Should you tell her or should I?" Callie asked.

Andrea smiled. "I think you should."

Once Chaos and Micah settled down, Andrea called to Micah as they sat on the couch. "Honey, come over here a moment. Miss Callie wants to tell you something."

Micah immediately got up and walked over to Callie. "Is everything all right?" Her wide blue eyes showed concern.

"Everything is fine." Callie tucked a strand of hair behind Micah's ear. "You see, I have to work so much these days that Chaos has been lonely. I'm very sad because he spends most of his days alone."

Micah turned a sad face to Chaos and nodded.

"Well, I've been thinking how much fun he would have if he could spend his days with you."

Her wide eyes just grew wider. Excitement practically exploded on her face.

"Do you mean—" Micah jerked around to look at her mom, who was smiling and nodding, then turned back to Callie.

"Yes, honey, your mom and dad agreed, and I'm going to give Chaos to you."

She let out a loud squeal and jumped up and down. Chaos joined her in the fun, barking and jumping about. Despite the pain in Callie's heart, she knew she was doing the right thing. She had no doubt whatsoever that Chaos would be happy in this home.

"I know this isn't easy for you," Andrea said. "You're more than welcome to come by any time to visit Chaos."

"Thank you, Andrea. I truly appreciate that. I know he will be happy here."

"You have shown the greatest love of all."

Callie looked up at Andrea.

"Sacrificial love. The kind that says I'm putting my own wants aside so you will have a better life," Andrea continued.

Callie's breath stuck in her throat. She knew Andrea was talking about Chaos but the comment hit her hard. All these years she had blamed her father, resented him and at times loathed him. But maybe he truly had left her for her own good.

The possibility made her heart freer than she'd ever felt before. A tiny sliver of hope ran through her veins, and she knew that whether she ever saw her dad again, she would be all right. She would cling to the idea that perhaps he truly did love her and gave her his best—and if that wasn't the case, she would forgive him anyway. Because that's what true love did. It offered forgiveness.

Giving up, letting go, setting free, putting her own wants aside so someone else could be happy—that was the person she wanted to be.

Now the question was did she love Brad Sharp enough to set him free?

Stepping out of the air-conditioned salon, Callie groaned at the stifling summer heat. This weather, especially on a Monday, definitely called for a stroll over to the ice-cream parlor for a chocolate shake. She glanced at the giant tubs along the walkway that exploded with colorful petunias, roses and daisies. Honeysuckle vines spilled from a nearby fence. Their fragrance mingled with the nectar of roses and perfumed the air.

Callie loved Burrow in the summer. Truly, she

loved every season. Each one brought its own thrill to her, and she had to experience them all.

The bell jingled softly as Callie stepped inside the parlor. The chilled air not only kept the ice cream in check, but also brought much relief to Callie. Though she loved the summer, she was not a huge fan of sweating.

"Hi, Callie," Olivia called out.

"How's the ice-cream girl?" Callie stepped up to the counter.

"Doing great."

Callie placed her order for a chocolate shake, and Olivia made it for her.

"Here you go," Olivia said, handing her the shake.

Callie grabbed her straw and took a drink. "Mmm, this is delicious. Good job, Olivia."

The teenager beamed. Just as Callie was trying to figure out how to ask about Brad, Olivia said, "Have you talked to Uncle Brad since he got back?"

Disappointment filled Callie's chest. She didn't even know Brad had come home. She had hoped he would contact her, but it wasn't as though he had to check in with her.

"No—no, I haven't."

Olivia slumped. "Oh, I thought he would call you." She shrugged. "Oh, well. I'm sure he will soon enough."

Callie smiled. Girls at that age were hopeless romantics. No need to burst her bubble.

"Did he have a nice time?" Callie considered asking if he had made a decision, but she didn't. In not knowing, she held on to hope.

Olivia thought a moment. "I guess so. Dad talked to him on the phone for a little while." She gazed out the window. "I can't imagine having the ocean nearby." She turned to Callie. "No wonder he's excited about it."

He was excited? Callie's mood headed south at record-speed. "Yeah, I'm sure it's beautiful." Callie looked into her cup. Unfortunately, her shake had lost its appeal.

"Sure beats Burrow," Olivia said with a laugh.

Her comment hit Callie like a punch to the abdomen, making it hard for her to breathe. "Well, I guess I'd better be going. I have a lot to do tonight."

"Better not get too busy. Uncle Brad might be calling, you know." She winked.

"I'll keep that in mind." Callie smiled and walked away.

Once she was out of view, Callie tossed her shake into a nearby trash bin. She didn't have the stomach for it. She'd lost her appetite somewhere between learning that Brad was home and hearing Olivia say that he might call her.

She had to face the raw truth. If he loved her,

truly loved her, he would have called her by now. Instead, he was avoiding her. That could mean only one thing.

Brad was moving to Belize.

A week ago today Brad had returned to Burrow with a major decision ahead of him. It had been a week of agonizing prayer, gut-wrenching honesty, laying everything on the line, begging God for direction. A bolt of lightening didn't cut through the clouds and spell out the answer. He didn't receive a postcard from Heaven. The Scriptures gave him food for thought, but no absolutes.

But the more he prayed about it, the more he learned about himself. He had blamed himself for Nicole's death. And he'd blamed others. It was time to let it go and forgive—others as well as himself. Not only that, but he needed to stop comparing himself with his brother. Ryan was a successful judge because he chose that path. Brad chose carpentry. Choosing a different direction did not make him a loser; it made him independent. And though Ryan had encouraged him to go to college, he had never belittled his choice. Brad could see now it was his own insecurity that had made him want to run to faraway places.

Going to Belize would be a great choice but for the wrong reasons. He needed to serve God wherever that would lead him, but more important, he needed to serve for the right reasons.

Those revelations brought healing and peace to his soul, which then settled the decision in his mind.

He would stay in Burrow.

Besides, just because he chose to work in Burrow didn't mean he couldn't occasionally go on a trip to help out.

Staying away from Callie all week had been an exercise in discipline. The past two weeks had been the longest weeks of his life. He hungered to see Callie like a man starved for food. But he hadn't wanted her presence to sway him one way or the other. He didn't want to fill either one of them with false hope until he knew the direction he would take.

It had been risky, no doubt. He could not imagine what she thought of him by now—or if she thought of him at all.

Still, he wanted to see her. Needed to see her. To explain his decision and to learn what that meant for them—if anything, on her part.

He could only pray they had a future together, but whether they did, he decided to take the job with the city.

If it wasn't too late.

* * *

Callie's heart thumped hard against her ribs as her car edged closer to Brad's home. Why she was worried, she didn't know—he would never be home on a Saturday afternoon. Still, she didn't want him to see her. They both knew she never traveled in the country, especially near his house, without reason. Glancing at the corn, she wondered if that "knee-high by the fourth of July" thing still applied. The corn was much higher than that, so she supposed the farmers were happy.

The car idled at the stop sign, and her fingers thrummed on the steering wheel. Two more blocks.

Please, don't let him see me, she said to herself, not minding in the least if God listened in and answered.

She was greatly relieved to see Brad's car was gone and the house appeared closed up. No signs of Hammer, but he would likely be in the house.

Disappointment swept through her. She didn't want him to see her, but she had hoped for a teensy glimpse of him. A lot could happen in two weeks. Hair growth, shedding pounds, all that.

She felt foolish, like a teenager spying on her boyfriend. What had gotten into her? Brad had been missing in action since returning from Belize. Clearly he didn't want to see her. Maybe he was afraid to tell her his decision.

She'd been praying for him, but her prayers had been for herself, too. And it seemed God had a few things to discuss with her. For example, it was time she stopped depending on others for her happiness. Everything she needed could be found in Him. Man could disappoint and fail, but God never failed.

She learned something else, too. God was in control. He would be with all of them and see them through life's journey. Aunt Bonnie and Uncle George knew her love went deep for them, and no matter where life took her that love would never change.

For the first time in her life, Callie truly understood sacrificial love. She could go or stay wherever God wanted her, with or without Brad, and she would be okay. But now she knew that her love for Brad was strong enough to carry her away from Burrow, if they were supposed to be together.

Callie pulled her car into the grocery parking lot on her way home. The small heel on her shoe had broken at the salon, but she figured she wouldn't see anybody on a lazy Saturday afternoon. So she hobbled a little—who cared? Most people would be picnicking in the park or participating in some other fun summer activity. If her yogurt supply hadn't dwindled to one container, she might have put if off, but she had no choice.

She climbed out of her car and clip-clopped to the store entrance. The air inside the building was refreshing. Grabbing a cart, she was halfway down the aisle when the wheel started squeaking. A groan escaped her. She had grabbed Rusty— that was her nickname for the cart—again. It seemed she had a knack for grabbing this cart. In fact, she'd used it so often she was sure she owned it. Everyone looked her way as she passed. Rusty had no problem drawing attention to himself—or maybe they were watching her hobble her way through the aisles on uneven heels.

Crossing the aisles to the dairy section, Callie stopped in her tracks when she spotted Brad reaching for a carton of eggs. Her heart flip-flopped while a butterfly convention settled in her stomach. The two weeks' hair growth looked good on Brad. She lingered a moment, then realized she needed to make a quick getaway before he saw her—what with that whole shoe thing and all.

Just as she turned her cart, Rusty squealed and Brad looked up.

"Callie, hi." He waved.

She waved back. They both stood there, transfixed in time, just staring at each other. Then Brad took bold, strong steps toward her. By the time he reached her, amusement lit his eyes and his lazy grin made her heart soar.

"Your foot okay?"

She lifted the heel of her shoe. "One of those days. Say, what are *you* doing grocery shopping?"

"I said I didn't cook—I didn't say I don't shop. A man's got to have food in the house."

She laughed. "I guess so."

His eyes gazed into hers. "I've missed you," he said.

Air tried to circulate in her chest. She could feel it swirling around, but it just couldn't seem to find her lungs. "I missed you, too," she managed.

"I want to tell you all about it. I had planned to call you today."

Breathe. Just breathe.

He took out a piece of paper and pen, wrote something, then handed it to her. "Meet me here tomorrow night at six-thirty. Can you do that—or do you have plans?" His eyes probed her face as though searching for something she wasn't saying.

"No, I don't have any plans." Great. She had just told him she had no life.

"So you'll meet me there?"

"Yeah."

"I need your advice on some colors for this house."

Her spirits dropped. This wasn't about being with her. It was about a house he was building.

"I'll take you out for a sandwich afterward, so come hungry."

She smiled, thinking that choosing paint and eating a sandwich didn't sound all that romantic. Which could only mean one thing.

He was going to dump her.

Chapter Nineteen

"Thanks for meeting me tonight, Ryan." Brad stirred some cream into his no-frills Americano. It suited him. Whipped cream, chocolate, flavorings—they only covered up the coffee taste, to his way of thinking.

Classical music played and Brad smiled, thinking of Callie asking him to the Philharmonic concert.

Ryan took a drink from his cup, then settled comfortably into his chair. "Glad to do it. It's been a while since we've had a heart-to-heart." Ryan watched him. "I take it you've made a decision about the job offer?"

Brad stared into his cup. "Yes."

"I'm listening."

He ran his hand through his hair. "This is all your fault, you know?"

Ryan's eyebrows shot up. A smile lifted at the corners of his mouth. "Oh?"

"Bringing Callie onto my job site when you could have had her serve time anywhere else in the city—" He stopped midrant and looked him straight in the eyes. "Why did you?"

"Why did I what? I thought we were talking about the job offer." Ryan held back a smile, and for a moment, Brad considered slugging him.

"Assign Callie to my job site?"

Ryan leaned forward, folded his hands together on the table and looked at Brad. "I knew she had been Nicole's friend. I also knew you had to work through some things concerning Nicole's death. I had hoped that Callie would help you do that."

His brother's concern took the fight right out of Brad. "You know, when we were growing up— after Dad died—I used to get really mad at you for being so overprotective. But I finally realized that's what I did with Nicole. I worried about her every move and wanted to protect her from everything. Then when she needed me most and I wasn't here, well, I couldn't come to terms with it."

"I get it, Brad. I really do. There's nothing I wouldn't do to help you get the life you truly want. I've always wanted the best for you. Sometimes I went a little too far, granted, but it was always with the best of intentions." Ryan shifted in his seat.

"I see that now, Ryan." Brad looked up. "Thanks."

"So, have you come to terms with it?"

Brad nodded. "After much prayer and soul-searching, I think I have—finally."

Ryan grinned. "Glad to hear it, little brother." He sat back. "Now, about that job offer?"

"I'm going to take it."

Ryan's brow furrowed. "Which one?"

"The one in Burrow."

Ryan broke into a full-fledged grin. "Hey, Brad, that's great. I'm so glad to hear that."

The look of genuine pleasure on his brother's face encouraged Brad. He appreciated how Ryan had waited patiently for his answer. He felt as if their relationship had finally shifted somehow.

Then Ryan leaned into the table and said, "Where does this leave you and Callie?"

Brad grinned. "Wouldn't you like to know."

"I really wish you would let me throw you an anniversary bash," Callie said to her aunt and uncle over lunch on Sunday.

"Pass the potatoes, will you?" Uncle George asked.

Aunt Bonnie obliged. "I know, dear. But honestly we've never enjoyed attention like that. Have we, honey?"

"We sure haven't. Makes me uncomfortable."

He scooped so many potatoes on his plate that Callie wondered if there would be any left.

"Well, then you won't mind my gift to you."

They both looked at her and she smiled, handing a bag to Aunt Bonnie.

"But it's not our anniversary until next week," Aunt Bonnie said, taking the bag from Callie.

"I know, but I wanted you to have this ahead of time." Callie's heart nearly thumped out of her chest. For years she'd been wanting to do something really special for them, and after all her hard work, plus the money Gram gave her, she was finally able to do it.

When Bonnie pulled out the envelope, she looked at her husband. "Look, it's an envelope, George."

"Uh-huh, that's what it is, all right," he mumbled between bites of potatoes.

Bonnie nudged him with her arm. "Oh, you." She opened the envelope and once she spotted the airline tickets, she squealed. In all her years, Callie had never heard her aunt squeal. Not once.

George dropped his fork. "Now, look what you made me do."

Wide-eyed, jaw unhinged, she handed the envelope to her husband. "She's sending us to Hawaii."

Uncle George choked on his potatoes.

* * *

Callie noticed Brad's truck in the driveway but rechecked the address on her paper anyway. How odd. This house appeared larger than the homes Brad normally constructed. The new subdivision had three other homes besides this one. Maybe this was one of Brad's side projects.

Pulling her car into the driveway, she shut off the engine and walked up to the door. With her being so new to the building business—that thought in itself made her chuckle—she wondered why he would want her opinion about anything. Though she had to admit she was pretty good with colors. On fingernails or walls, it made no difference to her. She knew a good color when she saw one.

She knocked on the front door. Was that music she heard? Maybe Brad was listening to music while he worked. Footsteps approached the door.

"Hi." The sight of him melted her, as always. She stepped inside and he pulled her into a long hug. He whispered into her hair, "It is so good to see you again."

To say that greeting surprised her was an understatement. She'd take it, though. Was he setting her up for the big news of his move? He was excited and probably assumed she would be, too.

Lord, please help me to be happy for him, wherever You lead him.

He pulled back and looked at her, his hands cupping her shoulders. "You should have seen Belize, Callie. It was incredible." Uh-oh, here it came. He was definitely setting her up. Her stomach sank and she hardly noticed the unpainted drywall and cement floors. But as he led her to the kitchen, she did notice a pleasing aroma in the air.

"What is that smell?"

He walked over to a crockpot, pulled the lid off and took a pleasurable whiff. "Beef stew." His hand swept sideways, pulling her gaze to a corner table with candlelight and linens.

She stared at him.

"Surprised?" he asked.

"Confused." She dare not hope this setup was for her—for them.

He walked across the concrete floor and pulled the chair out by the table.

She still stared at him.

"Um, this is where you would sit down."

In a zombielike state, she walked over to him and sat down in the waiting chair. She watched as he scurried to the kitchen, lifted chilled bottled waters from an ice chest and then scooped beef stew into deep soup bowls. She had to admit, even though he was preparing her for the worst, he didn't have to go to all this trouble.

Once the French bread was cut and placed on the table, along with the stew and drinks, Brad grabbed Callie's hand and prayed over their meal. Her brain was numb with disbelief and she hardly heard a thing.

When he finished, he picked up his spoon. "I hope you appreciate this meal. It's my first attempt at cooking, you know."

The reality of what he had said nearly bowled her over. "You made this meal?"

"Yep. Well, okay, Mom came over and guided me just a little."

Callie stared at him. Again.

"All right, it was a meal in a bag and all I had to do was cook it in the crockpot, but still."

She laughed. "I'm flattered. Truly."

Pleasure glowed from him. "You are?"

"Yes, I am." She swallowed hard and gathered the courage to ask her next question. "To what do I owe this honor?" Did she really want to know now, before their lovely meal was over?

"Well, I haven't talked to you since my trip to Belize, and I thought this would be a nice private way to do so."

She looked around at the unfinished walls and laughed. "If you wanted privacy, why not go to your house?"

"I told you, I needed your help with colors."

"I have to admit I was surprised by the house. It's quite a bit more elaborate than your usual ones."

He coughed. "Um, yeah. I'll tell you more about that later. For now, let me fill you in on Belize."

He told her about the country, the beauty of the setting, the ministry, his prayer time—and how he'd decided not to go. It took a moment for it to sink in.

"Callie, did you hear what I said? I'm staying in Burrow to take that job Ryan talked to me about."

"But don't you want to go to Belize?"

"I thought I explained that. My struggle with God, the surrendering, all that?" He glanced at his watch, rose from his chair and walked over to her, extending his hand. She took it and he raised her to her feet. "I want you to see this house."

Brad walked her from room-to-room, asking her what she thought would look good on the walls, where she might see furniture going in each particular room, getting her insights on decorating. By the time they were finished, they were back in the kitchen.

He faced her and took both of her hands into his. "Callie, I know this may seem crazy, but please don't say anything until I'm finished."

"Okay." She didn't have a clue where this was going, but she liked the feel of his hands over hers. And the look on his face told her good things were ahead….

"I brought you here and made dinner because I wanted to show you that sometimes we do the things we think we can't because love compels us. Oh, I know the dinner was a little thing, but I wanted to show you that I love you and I'm willing to go the extra mile to make you happy."

"Wait, Brad, if you're telling me that you're staying in Burrow because of me—"

He put his fingers against her lips. "Let me finish, okay?"

She nodded.

"I feel confident that Burrow is where I'm supposed to be—for now. Maybe for always. But the other thing I learned while I was gone is that I can't live without you. Your image followed me every moment. I could not get you out of my mind." He leaned closer. "I love you, Callie Easton. I have loved you from the day I first set eyes on you at the bakery and you ordered that ridiculous fat-free muffin." He searched her face. "Tell me you feel the same way." His eyes pleaded; his voice held hope and longing.

She smiled up at him. "Yes, Brad, I love you, too." He let out a sigh and pulled her close to him.

"I know how you feel about Burrow. I have

plenty of work I can do right here. And maybe once a year I could help out on a short-term mission trip." The words rumbled in his chest as she leaned against him. He pulled away and looked at her again. "What do you think?"

"If that's what you want to do."

"Would you go with me?"

She nodded. "I've learned a little about the agape love myself."

"Oh yeah?"

"It's a sacrificial kind of love. And that's the love I have for you. I'd be willing to go where we need to go, as long as we're together. That's how I know I love you." He pulled her close once again.

"So, Callie, a friend of mine started this house but ran into some financial trouble. I came over and took a look at it, liked what I saw and thought maybe you would, too."

She puzzled at what he was saying.

Then he pulled something out of his pocket. He knelt down on one knee, her hand in his, and said, "Callie, I want to live here in this house—with you." He flipped open the little black case and revealed a beautiful oval-shaped solitaire diamond. "Will you marry me?"

Tears slid down her face. "Yes. Yes, I will marry you!"

A huge grin broke out on Brad's face. He scooped her into his arms and swung her around, both of them laughing together. When he finally put her down, they were breathless. He tenderly slipped the ring onto her finger, pleased at the perfect fit. He leaned in and claimed his bride-to-be, kissing her face, her ears, her hair. "I've waited for you all my life. I guess big brother really did know best."

She snuggled into his shoulder. "I think Nicole would be pleased."

He squeezed her tightly. "I know she would."

How long she stood wrapped in his embrace Callie didn't know. What she did know is that she didn't want this night to ever end.

A honk sounded outside the door. "Who would that be?" she asked.

Brad glanced at his watch. "Oh, man, I forgot!"

"Forgot what?"

"Grab your bag or we'll be late for the concert."

She looked at him. "Concert? What concert?"

"The Philharmonic."

"But I thought you said you'd never go to one of those concerts."

"If there's one thing I've learned in the past few months it's that a person should never say *never.*"

She laughed and pulled her sweater around her

shoulders. He closed the door behind them and hugged her close to his side as they made their way to the black limo waiting at the end of the drive.

Callie glanced at the beautiful home that would one day be hers and Brad's, then back at the limo. "Please tell me this thing won't turn into a pumpkin at midnight. Because for the first time in my life, I feel like a princess."

He pulled her close. "You are a princess, baby. My princess." His hand brushed against her handbag and knocked it to the floor.

"Oh, I'm sorry." He reached down to pick it up for her. A paper had fallen out.

"Whoa. Isn't this a parking ticket?"

She snatched it from his hand. "Just trying to get a head start on my next building project."

"I think we should frame it."

They both laughed and took their first steps toward their future—as God had intended all along—together.

* * * * *

Dear Reader,

I have to confess I have far too much in common with Callie Easton when it comes to losing things. Fortunately, I've never been hauled off to jail or had to do community service. Though I'm happy to say that for Callie things seemed to work out.☺

You undoubtedly noticed that Callie and Brad didn't start off in the best of circumstances, but fortunately, it all worked out in the end.

Of course, this is fiction, and life isn't always like that. Sometimes things work out the way we hope and other times not. But the good news is that God is in control, and He works all things together for the good of those who love Him. Did you get that? Not necessarily the way we want but always for our good.

I've had disappointments in my life, as I'm sure you have, too. But God has never failed me. Not ever. For you see, no matter what I go through, He is always right there beside me, guiding, guarding, encouraging, getting me through.

Callie wanted desperately to reconnect with her dad and that never happened. She had to learn to accept things as they were, forgive and move on.

Brad learned to let go of his own ambitions, admirable as they were, and trust God with his future.

Sometimes we get so busy doing the "good things" that somehow we forget to stop and talk to God along the way, making sure we're still on the right track, doing the work He has called us to do.

We can't always see our way clear in a situation, but God can! When life's disappointments come, trust Him. When confusion settles in, trust Him. When all hope seems gone, trust Him! He will see you through!

Scatter Joy!

Diann Hunt

QUESTIONS FOR DISCUSSION

1. Callie Easton's life was out of control. Her organizational skills, or lack thereof, were only part of the problem. Does your life ever feel that way? How do you deal with it? Can you think of a better way of handling things?

2. Community service was not part of Callie's plans. She had a life to live, after all. Have you ever had an interruption to your life that upset your plans? What did you learn from it?

3. Brad Sharp thought he had his life all mapped out. Building homes for needy people overseas seemed a worthwhile ministry. But he soon discovered that God had a different plan for his life. Have you had a time in your life when you were on one path and you later realized that God had a different journey in mind for you? What did you do about it?

4. Callie's father abandoned her when she was young, which made it hard for her to trust others. And though her aunt reminded her that

God would never leave or forsake her, Callie had her doubts. Have you ever doubted God's presence?

5. Though Callie hoped to one day reconnect with her father, it never happened. She was disappointed, but she learned to leave the outcome to the Lord. Is there someone in your past with whom you want to reconnect? Things don't always work out the way we want, but God is still in control. Are you trusting Him with the relationships in your life?

6. Brad struggled with the death of his sister and letting go of self-imposed guilt. Is there guilt in your own life that you've brought before the Lord but can't seem to find victory over?

7. Brad couldn't control his sister. Brad's brother, Ryan, couldn't control Brad. Callie couldn't control her father. At some point in life we all learn that we have to "let go" of life's worries and trust God. Is there something in your life that you're struggling to surrender to God?

8. Callie and Brad hadn't foreseen that little Micah would have a part in bringing them

together. Is there someone whom God is using in your life to bring you closer to Him—or are you perhaps that someone in the life of someone else?

9. Callie's aunt and uncle took her in and loved her as their own. They generously welcomed her into their open arms and offered her a life far different than the one that could have been. God stands ready to do the same for us—take us in as His own and offer us a new life. Have you accepted His lavish gift? If not, what's stopping you?

10. God may lead you to faraway places, or He may show you that He has you where you are for a reason. Are you chasing dreams, or have you bloomed where you've been planted? You are here for such a time as this. What are you doing about it?

Dumped via certified letter days before her wedding, Haley Scott sees her dreams of happily ever after crushed. But could it turn out to be the best thing that's ever happened to her?

Turn the page for a sneak preview of
AN UNEXPECTED MATCH
by Dana Corbit,
book 1 in the new
WEDDING BELLS BLESSINGS *trilogy,*
available beginning August 2009
from Love Inspired®

"Is there a Haley Scott here?"

Haley glanced through the storm door at the package carrier before opening the latch and letting in some of the frigid March wind.

"That's me, but not for long."

The blank stare the man gave her as he stood on the porch of her mother's new house only made Haley smile. In fifty-one hours and twenty-nine minutes, her name would be changing. Her life, as well, but she couldn't allow herself to think about that now.

She wouldn't attribute her sudden shiver to anything but the cold, either. Not with a bridal fitting to endure, embossed napkins to pick up and a caterer to call. Too many details, too little time and certainly no time for her to entertain her silly cold feet.

"Then this is for you."

Practiced at this procedure after two days back in her Markston, Indiana, hometown, Haley reached out both arms to accept a bridal gift, but the carrier turned and deposited an overnight letter package in just one of her hands. Haley stared down at the Michigan return address of her fiancé, Tom Jeffries.

"Strange way to send a wedding present," she murmured.

The man grunted and shoved an electronic signature device at her, waiting until she scrawled her name.

As soon as she closed the door, Haley returned to the living room and yanked the tab on the paperboard. From it, she withdrew a single sheet of folded notebook paper.

Something inside her suggested that she should sit down to read it, so she lowered herself into a floral side chair. Hesitating, she glanced at the far wall where wedding gifts in pastel-colored paper were stacked, then she unfolded the note. Her stomach tightened as she read each handwritten word.

"Best? He signed it *best?"* Her voice cracked as the paper fluttered to the floor. She was sure she should be sobbing or collapsing in a heap, but she felt only numb as she stared down at the offending piece of paper.

The letter that had changed everything.

"Best what?" Trina Scott asked as she padded

into the room with fuzzy striped socks on her feet. "Sweetie?"

Haley lifted her gaze to meet her mother's and could see concern etched between her carefully tweezed brows.

"What's the matter?" Trina shot a glance toward the foyer, her chin-length brown hair swinging past her ear as she did it. "Did I just hear someone at the door?"

Haley tilted her head to indicate the sheet of paper on the floor. "It's from Tom. He called off the wedding."

"What? Why?" Trina began, but then brushed her hand through the air twice as if to erase the question. "That's not the most important thing right now, is it?"

Haley stared at her mother. A little pity wouldn't have been out of place here. Instead of offering any, Trina snapped up the letter and began to read. When she finished, she sat on the cream-colored sofa opposite Haley's chair.

"I don't approve of his methods." She shook the letter to emphasize her point. "And I always thought the boy didn't have enough good sense to come out of the rain, but I have to agree with him on this one. You two aren't right for each other."

Haley couldn't believe her ears. Okay, Tom wouldn't have been the partner Trina Scott would have chosen for her youngest daughter if Trina's grand matchmaking scheme hadn't gone belly-up. Still, Haley hadn't realized how strongly her mother disapproved of her choice.

"No sense being upset about my opinion now," Trina told her. "I kept praying that you'd make the right decision, but I guess Tom made it for you. Now we have to get busy. There are a lot of calls to make. I'll call Amy." Trina dug the cell phone from her purse and hit one of the speed dial numbers.

Haley winced. In any situation, it shouldn't have surprised her that her mother's first reaction was to phone her best friend, but Trina had more than knee-jerk reasons to make this call. Not only had Amy Warren been asked to join them downtown this afternoon for Haley's final bridal fitting, but she also was scheduled to make the wedding cake at her bakery, Amy's Elite Treats.

Haley asked herself again why she'd agreed to plan the wedding in her hometown. Now her humiliation would double as she shared it with family friends. One in particular.

"May I speak to Amy?" Trina began as someone answered the line. "Oh, Matthew, is that you?"

That's the one. Haley squeezed her eyes shut.

* * * * *

*Will her former crush be the one
to mend Haley's broken heart?
Find out in AN UNEXPECTED MATCH,
available in August 2009
only from Love Inspired®.*

Love Inspired®

SUSPENSE
RIVETING INSPIRATIONAL ROMANCE

These contemporary tales
of intrigue and romance
feature Christian characters
facing challenges to their faith...
and their lives!

**Four new Love Inspired Suspense titles are
available every month wherever books are
sold, including most bookstores, supermarkets,
drug stores and discount stores.**

Steeple
Hill®

Visit:
www.steeplehillbooks.com

HISTORICAL

INSPIRATIONAL HISTORICAL ROMANCE

Engaging stories of romance,
adventure and faith,
these novels are set in
various historical periods
from biblical times
to World War II.

NOW AVAILABLE!

Steeple
Hill®

For exciting stories that reflect traditional values,
visit:
www.SteepleHill.com